In Heaven's Shadow

In Heaven's Shadow

BOOK ONE: CITIZEN SOLDIER

MATTHEW BRYAN

iUniverse, Inc.
Bloomington

In Heaven's Shadow
Book One: Citizen Soldier

iUniverse books may be ordered through booksellers or by contacting:

iUniverse
1663 Liberty Drive
Bloomington, IN 47403
www.iuniverse.com
1-800-Authors (1-800-288-4677)

ISBN: 978-1-4759-8226-8 (sc)
ISBN: 978-1-4759-8228-2 (hc)
ISBN: 978-1-4759-8227-5 (ebk)

Printed in the United States of America

iUniverse rev. date: 03/21/2013

To my mom for showing me the path.
To my editor Annetta who shone a light for me to follow.
And to Adrienne, for walking with me and supporting me, even when I got lost.

I couldn't have got here without any of you.

CHAPTER ONE

The softly falling rain nearly masked the lonely squeak of a cart wheel as a woman slowly came into view. The rage of the storm, which just passed, left the street pooled with water, the oiled sheen of pollution glistening in the streetlights. She struggled along the sidewalk, working her way around the puddles and debris left in the storm's wake. Petite and obviously pregnant, she wrestled, pulling and tugging a small cart filled with cleaning supplies. She shuffled with the characteristic gait of an expectant mother as she labored down the street, head down, unaware of the tall figure watching her plight from high above.

His piercing blue eyes were calm as he gazed down on the city, his city. Standing in the light drizzle, short black jacket meeting jeans darkened by the rain, he looked like a typical thirty-year old. It was only the ethereal beauty of his face, almost too much for a man, which made him stand out. His shoulders twitched as water dripped down his back from his rain-slicked blond hair. For decades As'hame had watched this City of Angels grow, watched it expand and stretch its influence on a world slipping into corruption. Even after the long years of his existence and the numerous other cities he had watched over, he still marveled at this city and its attempts to shine; to be a beacon against the ever encroaching darkness. He loved this city and its people as he had no other city in his long life. That is why he stayed, that is why he walked the night, and that is why he killed.

His eyes grew cold as shadows stirred in the alleys below, and anger ignited his heart. He had been drawn here and now he knew why. The shadows broke free of the darkness and moved to surround the woman. As'hame, with a shake of his head, dropped from his perch. The natural grace of his kind was evident as he landed lightly in the shadows. The black biker boots he wore gave him sure footing as he strode with quick, smooth elegance to the alley mouth. The sight greeting him as he stepped onto the street fanned his anger, the muscles of his jaw jumping in his cheek. The woman stopped and faced the seven roughly dressed men, a proud tilt to her chin as they circled her, taunting.

"What are you doing out so late *chica*?" smirked a lanky man with a heavy beard.

"Looking for some company?" offered another through a mouth of blackened and rotted teeth.

"She has been looking for us, of course," the man behind her said quietly, causing her to spin and face him.

"Isn't that right? You walked the streets this night looking for us." The man's harsh voice grated as he stepped closer to her, the scar running from temple to chin standing stark against his tanned and weathered face.

She shook her head defiantly, fear apparent in her eyes, "I am just trying to get home."

Her voice cracked. As'hame saw her knuckles whiten as she clenched her cart. He hurried toward the group as the scarred man, obviously the leader, nodded for his companions to draw the circle closer. As'hame was close to enough now to sense their mortality and he realized this was not demon-driven torment. This was pure humanity: man's compassion, what made humans shine, matched only by their capacity for cruelty. As an As'rai, he routinely destroyed demonic possession wherever he found it but those disturbances, while increasing in recent months, never approached the number of times he encountered situations like this. Man preying upon man. The worst atrocities could not be blamed upon Hell but were solely the fault of man. And this angered him even as it threatened to bring him to his knees in overwhelming grief. Not free to indulge in either emotion, he clenched his jaw in restrained rage; large, strong hands closed tight in fists capable of punching through solid stone.

"You're going to be a little late." The coldness in the scarred man's voice dropped into the silence like a rock.

Her sudden scream broke in the air as the bearded man yanked the cart away and shoved her hard. She stumbled, almost falling, but managed to right herself and turned to face the scarred leader.

"Or very, very late. Right, Pete?" The man with rotted teeth leered as he came up behind the woman.

As'hame grabbed the man by his shoulder and waist, pivoting on his right foot, left foot sliding backwards, he pulled and flung the man to the ground.

"What the fuck!" Pete cried, the scar on his face twisting his mouth into a snarl. "John, get your ass up!"

The man, John, rolled over to his knees groaning, shaking his head in confusion.

"Help the clumsy idiot up, Tommy," Pete said pointing at John, "Theo, you grab her."

A short, fat man with greasy hair falling beneath an oil-stained Dodger's cap grabbed the woman roughly by the arms. He pulled her against him, licking the side of her neck, leaving a nasty slick trail across her skin.

As'hame shook his head as Tommy knelt by John trying to coax him to his feet.

"Come on, John, Pete'll kick your ass if you don't get up!" Tommy whispered urgently, tugging on John's arm.

Taking a step forward, As'hame set his left foot and punted John in the chest as he sat up. The force of the kick sent him crashing into Tommy and knocking them both sprawling.

"Piss on you then, John!" Tommy yelled struggling to get to his feet, "You can stand up on your own then, you fat bastard!"

"But it wasn't me!" John gasped where he lay on the ground, stunned by the force of the kick and the collision.

"Idiots!" growled Pete as he stepped around Theo and the woman. "Hold her, Theo. John, I've warned you about drinking too much. I'm going to teach you a lesson this time," he said, drawing a wicked looking knife from behind his back.

"No Pete! I haven't been drinking. Well, not much. Please, you don't have to do this!" John pleaded as he tried to scramble away.

As'hame ignored Pete and John. Slipping around them, he walked toward Tommy who stood watching, fear evident on his bearded face. Pete stalked toward John as As'hame came up on Tommy and struck him down with a hammer blow of his fist. Tommy slammed to the ground unconscious, and As'hame stepped over his supine body toward Theo and the woman he held.

"I can taste the fear on your skin," Theo whispered as As'hame drew near. "You don't even know what to fear, yet."

Theo appeared clueless to what was happening behind him so As'hame didn't bother with anything fancy. He simply stepped up and clubbed him down. The woman flinched as Theo fell to the ground and then slowly turned, her eyes passing over As'hame like he wasn't there. For a moment, he thought about revealing himself, something he rarely did with humans, but decided against it as he turned back to the gang members. Three of them down and the rest were still unaware. Not that it would have mattered. Even if they had looked around, they would not have been able to see him. They would have just seen three of their friends lying crumpled on the ground. As'hame was aware of the woman watching in shock; with a leaping front kick, he sent another assailant into the darkness of unconsciousness.

Mere seconds had passed. Pete had just reached John, who cowered against a brick wall by the mouth of the alley as As'hame approached.

"I've had enough of you not listening, John," Pete said, holding up his knife, its razor sharp edge glinting in the light.

This has gone on long enough. Grabbing Pete's outstretched arm, As'hame twisted it up behind the man's back. The knife fell from Pete's nerveless fingers as As'hame twisted it hard, no sympathy in him for the cruel and barbaric leader. As'hame saw the looks of fear on the others as he spun sharply and flung the leader against the brick wall. Pete hit the wall hard, the crack of his shoulder breaking audible in the air.

"Oh God!" Pete shrieked as he fell to his knees, clutching at his broken shoulder.

As'hame ignored Pete, who knelt looking around the street in shock. John's eyes were huge over his crooked and broken teeth, shock and fear apparent on his face as As'hame slipped past him. He walked to where the two remaining men stood, their gazes flipping from Pete to Tommy to each other. The look of confusion on their faces brought a little joy to As'hame and he mentally flipped a coin. No one but the woman had noticed the fate of the others but they all noticed as he buried a booted foot in the stomach of the man on the right. The thug lifted off his feet and folded around As'hame's leg before collapsing to the ground gasping for breath. That seemed to be the last straw for the remaining gang member who turned and ran down the street. As'hame shrugged and let him go as he turned back to where Pete and John sat against the wall.

"What the hell is going on, John?" Pete whispered, fear lending a rasp to his voice.

"How would I know?" John said.

As'hame knelt and released his voice. "If either of you continue with this unacceptable behavior, you will find out."

5

He paused and allowed his anger to color the next words he spoke. "And this will not be an experience you will enjoy, or likely survive."

Both John and Pete blanched at hearing the disembodied voice threatening them. John pushed himself to his feet and made to walk away.

"Wait! John, please, you can't leave me here. Please, help me!" Pete pleaded, holding out his hand to the man he had terrorized moments ago.

"Seriously?" John shook his head.

"Please? I'm sorry. I was only trying to scare you."

Pete's begging must have had an effect because, as As'hame watched, a small quirk touching his lips, John leaned down and pulled Pete to his feet. *Perhaps there is still hope for that one.* He watched John and Pete stagger together down the alley before they disappeared into the darkness.

As'hame finally looked back toward the woman, expecting to discover she had fled the alley. He was mildly surprised to see her standing in the same spot, as though rooted. He marked the expression of confusion on her face as she looked at the unconscious bodies surrounding her. He smiled when she crossed herself and then carefully bent down and righted her cart, picking up and repacking the few items that had fallen free. She looked around shaking her head and then continued on her way, weaving her way among the men outstretched around her. As'hame laughed out loud when, as she passed by the single conscious member, still on his hands and knees, she kicked him hard in the side of the head.

She is definitely a survivor. He watched her continue down the street. The squeak of the cart wheel echoed into the air, slowly fading until it was lost in the night.

"You enjoyed that a little much, don't you think?"

The sibilant voice coming from the darkness chased the smile from As'hame's face, and he turned to face the alley mouth as shadow sauntered into the light.

CHAPTER TWO

I came here looking for you," the figure said, stepping forward.

As'hame studied the form for a moment, its scaled skin catching and reflecting the light.

"What purpose could a demon have with one of the As'rai, Mkai?" he asked quietly, "even one as patient as I?"

"I told you. I came here looking for you." Mkai said.

"Do not toy with me, demon." As'hame said, taking a step forward, "You and your kind have been thrown from this world time and time again. This city, as are so many others, is under the protection of the As'rai and, thus, under mine. You have no business here."

"I came here to share some news." Mkai said, "News you don't have."

"I doubt that any news you have would be of interest to me." As'hame shrugged his shoulders, suddenly massive with restrained power. "So why should I not send you back to the hell you crawled from?"

"Whoa!" Mkai said quickly, holding up both hands, black-tipped claws glossy in the light. "I didn't crawl from Hell. I was sent."

"Sent? You and the rabble like you are not errand boys. You have pride enough for that, at least."

"Even so, we were sent, the riffraff of Hell, as you would call us. You could easily send me back, but it would accomplish nothing. I hope you at least hear me out," Mkai said, his tone laced with sarcasm and something else.

Regret perhaps. As'hame nodded motioning Mkai to continue.

"We have a slight history, you and I. I have never fought against you and have never given you any trouble nor resisted when you've banished me." Mkai said, meeting As'hame's eyes, diffidence evident in his posture.

"That is the only reason I am giving you this moment," As'hame said, "this short moment, to explain what you are doing in my city."

"I thank you for that. May we go someplace else, someplace out of sight?" Mkai said, relief filling his voice, "It's worth my life to be seen with you. I'm risking everything telling you what I know."

The soft rain beat a tempo on the cars around them as As'hame studied Mkai quietly. His nervousness was evident and he almost looked scared, an emotion As'hame had never seen from a demon before. *It is unsettling to see a demon in such a state.*

"Very well. Can you make it to the top of that building?" As'hame broke the silence and pointed at a four story building a couple blocks away.

"Yes. If I can't pick the locks to get to the stairs, I'll climb the outside."

"I will wait for you there." As'hame said, rolling his shoulders, wings suddenly stretching out behind him, "Be quick."

A leap and a quick thrust of his wings sent him into the air. His wings gleamed silver in the moonlight streaming through the scattering clouds as he soared toward the building. Moments later, his boots thumped onto the roof. He turned and watched Mkai slipping down the street, staying to the shadows when he was able. *He really is worried. It must be something important.* The rain tapered off to a light sprinkle, clouds starting to break up, as the faint sounds of Mkai climbing the fire escape reached As'hame's ears.

"We are hidden from watchers, and I should hear anyone seeking to climb the fire escape after you," As'hame said when Mkai finally made his way to the roof, "Speak, and quickly, for I am tiring of this."

"I will tell you everything I know. That is why I'm here," Mkai said, crouching down in the shelter of the wall, "But I have a question, if you would indulge me."

A raised eyebrow was the only reply As'hame offered, so Mkai continued, "Do you reveal yourself to those you save?"

"What purpose would that serve? We are not here to make friends; we are here to protect them," As'hame said with a shrug, "Why would you ask such an odd question at a time like this?"

"What about that woman?" Mkai said, ignoring the question, "She has no idea what just happened, does she?"

"No she does not, but it does not matter. Her mind will make up something to explain it all. I do not show myself to the humans I protect. Again, why does that interest you?"

"I've often wondered. We demons don't have the power the As'rai still enjoy. We can't hide from them the way you do, all we can do is use illusion to appear human. I have long wondered what it was like to be invisible to them."

As'hame shook his head, "It is the way it is; it is irrelevant. Now tell me why you risked so much to approach me."

"Very well," Mkai said, "But please remember I am risking not simply your punishment. If Hell knew what I was doing they would move mountains to kill me."

"I have not forgotten. Speak."

"You probably haven't heard but there is a new game in town. I told you I was sent. Not just me, but every demon that can walk, crawl, skitter or fly. All of us, sent for one purpose. To corrupt Man," Mkai said, looking directly at As'hame.

"Why now? Why would Samael start pushing now?" As'hame said.

"But Samael isn't who sent us. He's been overthrown." The words fell quietly.

As'hame studied Mkai crouching before him, and struggled to hide his shock while he thought through the implications.

"Someone has taken over Hell from Samael? Who would dare? Or have the power? He was from the first rank of archangels before he was thrown from Heaven for his sins." As'hame finally said.

"I haven't been able to figure that out yet. She came out of nowhere, threw him down, and chained him and his first generals. She now rules," Mkai whispered.

"What? She? Hell is now ruled by a female demon?"

"Yes. She calls herself Kalia and, if anything, she's even harsher than Samael ever was. He was pushed into a role he never wanted. She chose this and seems to delight in the punishment of others. Any soul, or demon for that matter, to which she turns her gaze is visited with torments greater than any Samael ever devised." Mkai's eyes darted to the shadows.

He returned his gaze to As'hame. "And that's the second thing I was able to discover. It's the catalyst prompting me to seek you out," he said quietly. "She's not just tormenting the lost souls, punishing them for their sins. She's torturing souls with the express purpose of conversion. She's recruiting an army. An army not of demons, but the souls of the damned."

"An army? An army of the damned, but why? What could she possibly . . ." As'hame trailed off as his mind fastened on the only reason possible.

"That's right." Mkai said filling the silence, "She's building an army to wage war on God. She is planning on picking up where Samael failed. She is going to storm Heaven with an army of God's favorites, with the belief He won't destroy them."

As'hame stared out across the city, stunned. The minutes dragged by, neither demon nor angel speaking, the rain filling the silence.

As'hame finally turned his troubled gaze to Mkai. "It could very well work. It would make Him pause a moment, for sure. He created man in his image, en-souled with the power of His love for them. He will not destroy the souls with which He gifted them."

"It gets worse," Mkai murmured.

"How could it get worse?"

"God's done it again. He's giving Mankind another chance. He's sent His Son to earth again to save them."

His words fell into the silence like stones into a pond, the sudden stop in the falling rain adding unneeded weight.

"You didn't know?" Mkai said, looking at the stunned expression on As'hame's face.

"No. We have not been in contact with Heaven since the War," As'hame said, shaking his head.

"That's the secondary mission Kalia issued. Find him. Few, and I mean very few, of us know why. I overheard a discussion I wasn't supposed to. She's looking for him. Somewhere out there, God's son sits waiting to be found." Mkai swept his arm across the city, "He has no idea who he is, and her goal is to find him, to take him, and to convert him to her side before he's ready."

"And He will lead her armies to war against His Father," As'hame finished quietly.

"Exactly. And that's why I came to you. I want no part of another war, but if it's coming, I want to be on the side of good. I chose wrong last time, and this is my chance to make that right."

As'hame gazed out on his city, the beauty of the freshly fallen rain tainted by the knowledge just learned, making his heart ache. The fragrance of new rain had always been one of his favorite scents but it soured in his nostrils at the thought of what was to come.

"I cannot promise anything, Mkai," As'hame said, turning to face his enemy-turned-ally. "But regardless of what is decided by my leaders, the news you have brought me, the risks you have taken, have earned you a friend."

Mkai smiled up at As'hame with relief. "Who would ever have thought this could happen, angel and demon . . . friends."

"I need to get this information to my Council and there is little time," As'hame said, turning to leave the rooftop, "You can fill me in on as many details as you know while we travel."

"Wait, we have even less time than you think," Mkai said, stopping him with a hand on his shoulder.

As'hame turned slowly, "Why? What else have you not told me?"

"It's not just happenstance I came to you. Yes, we have history, you and I, but there's more." Mkai dropped his hand and looked around at the silent city.

"He's here. In Los Angeles. God decided there would be no better place for His Son to announce Himself than the city many blame for Man's fall into iniquity," Mkai said. "L.A., and all it stands for, has hastened Man's descent from His grace, but He also sees it as a beacon for good. His intent is to give Man a chance, using the world's focus on this City of Angels to bring them back to His light."

"His Son, here? In my city?" As'hame murmured, a tingling thrill of anticipation laced with fear slipping down his back.

"Yes, and He's defenseless and my kind know it."

"Oh, He is not defenseless, not completely," As'hame said, "He may be unaware of them, but His gifts are there, just dormant. They will react to defend Him. Plus, in a very short time, He'll have me," As'hame said with a tight grin, stretching his arms to his sides.

Mkai stepped back as, with a flash, As'hame appeared suddenly clothed in the Armor of Silver, longsword by his side, wings spread wide behind him. The clouds broke above them and the glow of the moon was mirrored as As'hame released the restraints on the inner glow, a part of every angel.

"You'll need more than an archaic weapon to win against what's coming." Mkai raised his hand and squinted against the sudden glare. "They will be using every modern piece of technology or weapon they can," Mkai said.

"Oh, I am not totally stuck in the past," As'hame said. He muted his inner light, noting the relief on Mkai's face, "I have not turned my back on the new world. We are not constrained from using firearms. While I am familiar with them, I prefer not to use them without great need. It is an idiosyncrasy that is shared with your kind, I believe."

"It is. We don't use modern weapons, usually, but for this they will. The old rules won't be honored this time." Mkai said, "We need to hurry. I don't know exactly where He is, His name, or even what He looks like, but at least they don't know anything either."

"It will make our job more difficult, but I have a trick you and your kind do not," As'hame said, striding to the edge of the roof. "I can feel God."

"But how will that help?"

"I will not be able to sense the Son strong enough to pinpoint His exact location but, if I cover the city, I should be able to find at least the area." As'hame said spreading his wings. "I will cover the city and try to pinpoint a rough location of where He is."

"Then what?" Mkai asked.

"If I can determine the area of the city He is in, I will come find you and we can search for Him together." As'hame said. "Once we find Him we will head to New York. My orders High Council is located there and they are best able to organize protection for him there. The trip itself will be the greatest danger, since we cannot fly Him there directly."

"But what about me?" Mkai said, "How can I help? I can't fly."

"We need equipment, a safe house, weapons, and a vehicle. It is a long trip from here to New York and the Council," As'hame said, turning to him. "I know your specialty. Can you arrange those things?"

Mkai paused a long moment. As'hame knew he was asking a lot of the demon as the warrior angel waited for his answer. Mkai's next words would determine if he was worth the trust As'hame was willing to give him.

At last, Mkai sighed, seeming to come to a decision. He looked As'hame in the eye. "Yes. This is my chance to make right a terrible choice. When you return, you will have what you need."

As'hame nodded. Redemption. He understood the concept well and his confidence in Mkai grew.

"I will be back when I get a rough idea where to start searching. Take my torc," As'hame said stepping up to the roof ledge and tossing Mkai a large silver ring. "I can use it to find you. Do not lose it."

Then, with a smile, he launched himself from the roof, his spread wings arcing him into the night sky.

CHAPTER THREE

As'hame was a distant shadow when Mkai finally turned away. For a moment, he paused and breathed deep of the life around him. He relished his time on Earth, in ways no demon should. The solace Mkai gathered to him from things as simple as rain in the treetops was a light for him, a balm through the long lonely years of his existence.

He studied As'hame's torc a moment; a thick, silver ring twisted to look woven, open on one end, a flat disc closing each side. Looking closer, he felt a thrill. The ancient emblem of the As'rai was embossed on each disc. As'hame had given him, a demon, the bracelet of his order. He fought a shiver of trepidation as he slipped it over his left wrist, half-surprised when it didn't burn him. He squeezed the ends tight and held his hand up, the silver bright in the moonlight. Mkai admired it for a moment and then dropped his arm, letting his coat sleeve fall over it. He turned from the edge, his mind already cataloging what he'd have to collect. Only then did he realize he wasn't alone any longer.

He raised his head and sniffed, looking around cautiously, scanning the shadows, suddenly deep with hidden dangers. A dog barked in the distance as an errant breeze, left over from the departed storm, brought a familiar scent.

"Come out, Rahale, I know you're there," Mkai said.

"Mkai, I was wondering why you hadn't shown up for the clan meeting," Rahale said, stepping out of the gloom. "But I never imagined this. Betraying us, my Lord. Why? You know what this is for." Rahale continued, walking closer. "Heaven. Heaven that has been denied us for too long. We have been cursed with these mal-shaped and deformed bodies, cast from His light. And it will all end. She will lead us to victory and He will have no choice but to accept us back to our rightful place or watch Heaven burn!"

Mkai saw the light of madness in Rahale's eyes, a common sight in Hell's demons. Rahale matched Mkai closely in appearance; boots and jeans with a simple t-shirt and coat. His scales were a dull bronze while Mkai's had a reddish hue. With their slender builds and even features, they could have been brothers, and were, of a sort. But the glow of fanatical insanity shining in Rahale's eyes was his alone.

"You're a fool Rahale," Mkai said, rolling his shoulders under his coat. "She wants war for her own means; it has nothing to do with us. And from what I've seen, her victory would be a disaster for all. Hell was balanced, organized, and had a purpose, though one you probably didn't recognize." He drew closer. "She has thrown all that away for her own selfish goals."

"You don't know what you're talking about! You're jealous. Jealous of those of us she honors! You who are nothing beneath her gaze."

"It matters not our disagreement here, Rahale," Mkai said quietly, shrugging out of his coat, "for you're not leaving this rooftop alive."

"Wait!" Rahale cried as Mkai leapt at him, "No! Don't!"

Rahale's cry was cut short as Mkai struck, knocking him to the ground. He rolled desperately to the side and half-rose to his knees. Mkai rushed in and felt the air whoosh out when Rahale lunged up desperately, catching him with his shoulder. Mkai staggered back, trying to suck in air while watching Rahale get to his feet, a wicked grin showing Rahale's pointed teeth. Mkai had only seconds to catch his breath before Rahale charged, his arms wide, black claws a dull glint. *Mistake.*

Mkai reached out as Rahale got within range and grasped his enemy's right wrist with his left hand. With a convulsive heave, he pulled Rahale over his shoulder and flung him across the roof. Rahale landed in a heap and struggled to get to his knees, shaking his head. Mkai stepped in carefully, wary of a trap. Sadness touched him for a moment at the pain in Rahale's eyes when their gaze met.

"I'm sorry it has to end this way. Once, eons ago, I did call you friend." Mkai said sadly, drawing a knife from his belt. "But that time passed long ago. You take delight in the suffering and torment of others, but I never did. I've hidden who I really am for far too long. This time I'm fighting on the right side, not just taking the easiest path."

Mkai stepped toward him and Rahale blanched.

"Before you die, tell me how you came so close. How did you approach without the As'rai sensing you?"

Rahale shook his head in refusal, his defiance slowly fading as Mkai stepped closer.

"Please! Mkai, we've known each other for so long, you don't have to do this." Rahale pleaded, sidling away, "You can let me go. I won't say anything, I promise!"

"How Rahale?"

"A ring!" Rahale blurted out, fear cracking in his voice. "Kalia gives them to her favorites. It blocks the cursed As'rai from sensing us."

"A ring? I've never heard of anything like that and I doubt the As'rai have either. You've earned a quick death for telling me. I can't give you more than that."

"But . . ." Rahale gasped, struggling to his feet, his arm clasped against his side.

"As much as you say otherwise, you couldn't keep secret the word of my defection. We both know it," Mkai said, sadly shaking his head. "This is not about you and me, it's so much more than that.

The world, Heaven and Hell both, all of it, rests on what was put in motion on this rooftop. I'm sorry, Rahale. I'll make it quick, that much I can do for you."

"No!" Rahale screamed and, turning, leapt from the rooftop.

The sound of his body crashing down through four stories filled the night air as Mkai rushed to look over the edge. He couldn't believe his eyes when Rahale staggered to his feet. Judging from the debris scattered on the street, Rahale had managed to break his fall by grasping the balconies so, when he crashed through the canopy over the entrance, the fall didn't kill him. He was obviously hurt, staggering like a drunk toward the safety of the alleys.

Mkai cursed and rushed for the stairs. He couldn't take the same route as Rahale and couldn't afford to let him get away. By the time he reached the ground, Rahale was nowhere to be found. From the amount of blood on the ground, Mkai could hardly believe the demon had managed to get up. It was almost enough to hope he'd die, lost in some alley. Mkai knew he couldn't count on it.

Glancing around, Mkai found the trail of blood leading into an alley. Mkai realized the danger if he followed Rahale into the alleys. Rahale had lived in Los Angeles for many years and would have places to hide and know where best to ambush someone following him. With a sigh, Mkai drew his dagger and entered the darkness. He didn't have a lot of time to search, but the mission was too important to risk Rahale spreading the news of Mkai's defection. His palms slicked with sweat as he slipped through the shadows, eyes roaming, scanning every possible hiding place. The black of the alley was too dense even for eyes accustomed to the gloom of Hell. Mkai might not be able to see the trail of blood but its scent was strong in his nostrils as he stalked through the trail of alleys. The scent grew stronger as he slowed down and approached a corner, eyes taking in everything.

His ears caught a faint scraping sound and he stood still, listening, straining, waiting to hear it again. The sound of a distant siren reached him where he waited, the barely audible hum of traffic breaking the silence. The scent of blood was almost overpowering and Mkai dropped to one knee. There was an almost indiscernible shine just to his right and, reaching out, he felt the stickiness of blood, its copper tang sharp in his nose when he lifted his hand. *Why has it pooled here? He must be nearby.*

The scrape sounded again and his senses screamed. He leaned forward, eyes searching the darkness. Almost too late, Mkai realized what his senses told him. Action followed thought and he leapt forward into a roll, twisting his body until he slammed up against a dumpster. Mkai's elbow went numb from the impact as an air conditioning unit crashed to the ground where he had been standing moments ago.

"Dammit!" Rahale's curse reached Mkai where he lay in the alley.

"Almost, Rahale!" Mkai called, rubbing his elbow as he stood. *Sneaky sonofabitch almost caught me with that stupid trick.*

"You're a fool, Mkai, to throw your existence away like this. She won't forgive you."

He almost sounds sad. The thought came unbidden and Mkai angrily shook his head. *Don't relax your guard you idiot, he's dangerous and your mission is too important.*

"Do you even wonder why I'm doing what I am?" Mkai asked, ears straining to hear his enemy. "Can you even grasp the reasons?"

"What can possibly be worth risking eternity?"

"Forgiveness. Do you ever let yourself remember Heaven? What it was like? Do you ever miss that?"

Silence was his only answer. *Maybe I can reach him or at least buy some time.*

"I made choices back then, same as we all did. But I have a chance now to make up for it. To maybe hear the Song of Heaven again."

"But she promises us Heaven!" Rahale called down and this time there was no mistaking the longing in his voice.

"Do you really think she can deliver on that promise? Samael didn't even come close, yet we all suffered for it. His actions, and their influence, resulted in us all being cast out. What makes you think she could accomplish what he couldn't? What do you think our punishment would be when she fails?"

"Her plan is brilliant! We can't fail. He would not destroy His children and has to let us in!"

"And if she's wrong? Or worse, partially right? What do you think would happen to Heaven when Hell invades? Do you really think the angels would be willing to stand beside us? Halo to horn, feathered wings to scaled? Now? After all this time? Don't be absurd. Even if she manages to bust through the gates of Heaven all that would result is a perpetual war, in Heaven, on earth, and in Hell. Worse than you could even imagine." Mkai's voice carried the certainty of doom through the air and he waited for Rahale's response.

Faint scuffing sounds reached his ears and he pictured Rahale standing and shifting from foot to foot.

"I would rather continue this lonely existence, or even forfeit it entirely, to stop that from happening," Mkai said and waited.

"I wouldn't!" Rahale screamed, "I'd rather see Heaven destroyed than continue on this way!"

Mkai stood and listened to Rahale's footsteps as he ran off.

"I won't let that happen." Mkai said quietly.

With a final shake of his head, Mkai sheathed his dagger and walked through the darkness. He sighed with regret, knowing that Rahale would spread the word about what happened. Soon Mkai would be hunted as well. Hell never accepted betrayal, even less now, and it would be better to take his own life than to be taken back alive. He knew the torment visited upon him would make him wish he'd never been created.

Since he first took breath, he'd craved a purpose for his life and now he'd finally found it. Finding God's Son. Nothing would shake him from his self-appointed task, nothing. With a final glance at the darkness, Mkai moved off, driven by his own mission. *I have a lot to do.* He slipped through the shadows, his hand twisting As'hame's torc where it rested on his wrist.

CHAPTER FOUR

The odor of onions and garlic filled the narrow, dingy hallway. Light from the broken window split the darkness into shadows as Mkai walked up the stairs, assuming his human glamour without a second thought. Stepping carefully over scattered debris and garbage, he made his way down the hallway to the only door left. Most abandoned buildings in this part of L.A. didn't last long before being stripped of everything useful. Doors were often the first thing stolen as they could be used for walls and roofs when necessary. The onion and garlic smell became almost overwhelming, masking the rancid reek of the hallway as he approached his destination. He stepped up to the door and paused; he heard off-key singing through the door and it made him smile.

Roger was one of Mkai's many contacts, but one of the few he actually liked. Though he was capable of gathering what he needed on his own, Mkai preferred working through humans, not only because it was easier, but also for the contact. Having them collect information and items for him gave the excuse to spend time with them, helped him learn more about their nature. The singing broke off as he softly knocked on the door. This entire floor of the abandoned apartment building had only one tenant but there was no need to advertise his visit if he could help it.

Moments later, the peephole darkened as the occupant gazed through it. He grinned and nodded. He heard the snick of first one, then two locks click open, then the slow grind of metal sliding on metal. Music filled the hallway as the door eased open a crack.

"H-hello?" Roger stuttered.

"It's me. We need to talk," Mkai said, moving his face into the light falling through the door.

Roger grinned, his yellowed teeth exposed for a moment as he nodded and closed the door. The chain rattled and he ushered Mkai inside. Mkai looked about the familiar room as Roger quickly checked the hallway and closed the door, relocking it.

"That's new." Mkai said as Roger slid a security bar across the door.

"Yes. This neighborhood has g-g-gone downhill." Roger waved Mkai to the worn-down and patched sofa. "It has been t-too long."

"Don't let me interrupt. Please, finish your meal," Mkai said, taking the offered seat and crossing his legs. "This is a surprise visit but I didn't have time to call."

"Th-thank you, my friend," Roger said, turning back to the small stove after cranking the volume down on the old radio sitting on the counter.

Mkai couldn't help but smile as he watched him in the kitchen. Roger puttered around, putting the final touches on his meal. He sprinkled on some salt and stirred the mess of sausage and onions. Standing in his kitchen in slippers, his worn khakis, patched New York Yankees sweatshirt with his grey hair a mussed tangle, Roger looked like any other old, retired man barely making a living on a pension growing smaller with each passing year. Mkai knew that wasn't true.

Once, years ago, during a late night conversation about the world, Roger had let it slip that he had thousands of dollars hidden away, in numerous locations. He didn't trust the banks, and, since his wealth didn't come through honest means, it was safer to avoid banks when he could. So he squirreled money away for the future. Mkai had asked him, when the neighborhood first started going so badly downhill, why he continued to live where he did.

"Th-this is my home. It has been for more years than I can count. I will not l-leave. It is safe enough."

Since then, each time Mkai came to see him, Roger had added new locks, or a solid steel door, always something to make his home more secure. The old man's refusal to leave his home was just another of his quirks. That and calling Mkai "friend". It was something Roger had done almost since the beginning of their relationship. Mkai let his thoughts go back through the many years they had known each other. Since their first meeting when Roger was still a young boy, theirs had been a relationship different than most of Mkai's other contacts. *I suppose you could call us friends.*

"Do you remember when we first met?" He asked as Roger gave a final stir and dumped the sausage and onions onto a plate.

Mkai watched Roger move from the kitchen and carefully settle on the torn chair across from him.

"Of course I do" Roger nodded with a grin, "I was so y-young."

"You were. You seemed very young to me, but already skilled with providing things not quite legal, shall we say."

"But you haven't changed," Roger said, "In all this t-time."

Mkai looked across at Roger as he slowly worked through his meal. In all the years he had involved himself with humans, only once had he held a conversation about his origins. It drove that man insane. *This will be different. It is a different time, more enlightened, with open talk of Heaven and Hell, of monsters and aliens. I hope.*

"You never asked why. I have appreciated that. Not having to lie to you has been one of the things making our . . . relationship different," Mkai began.

Roger opened his mouth to respond, a piece of sausage stuck in his teeth.

"No, you keep eating, my . . . friend. I have a lot to tell you."

Roger looked at Mkai, a concerned furrow appearing on his brow as he went back to eating.

"You have never asked about my past, and I've never volunteered more than necessary in all the years we've known each other. I'd like to say it was for your safety, the less you know, et cetera, but it wasn't just that." Mkai continued, leaning forward, "It was partly for your safety but mostly because you wouldn't have believed a word I said . . . or worse, maybe you would have believed."

Mkai paused, taking a deep breath, "I am not . . . human."

The words fell between the two, music filling the background, the scent of garlic and onion still strong in the air. Roger paused with his fork half-way to his mouth and looked long and hard at Mkai. Mkai returned his gaze as calmly as he could, while inside he thrilled to finally say those words out loud. The feeling of finally telling someone the truth brought an unexpected excitement to the conversation. There was too much danger involved in what was happening to not tell Roger everything.

Minutes passed, seeming like hours, before Roger completed the fork's journey, nodding at Mkai to continue as he started to chew.

"I've been on this earth for thousands of years. I was here when Man first walked upright. I've been here since the Great War in Heaven. Your Bible is partly correct. There was a war. Samael, or Lucifer, or Satan, as he is also named, was indeed cast out. As were a multitude of angels, those who either supported him or just didn't fight on God's side."

Mkai paused, letting Roger finishing chewing and swallowing.

"Are you . . ." Roger began, his eyes wide with apprehension and awe.

"I . . . was an angel. I, too, was cast from Heaven. I didn't directly rebel against my God, but in the end it didn't matter." Mkai shrugged.

"Demon?" Roger whispered, his hands beginning to shake.

"We are called that but I mean you no harm," Mkai said quickly raising his own hands, "There are many kinds of us, some harmless to Man. I collected information. I moved about, on earth and Heaven, in my quest. As it happened, those for whom I worked sided with Samael. I, because of my association with them, was banished with the rest," Mkai looked at the worn carpet at his feet.

"I won't claim to have been innocent. My actions did cause the destruction and death of my brethren. I was God's, to do with as He willed. I accepted His punishment."

Roger stood up suddenly and walked unsteadily to the kitchen. He scraped the food into the garbage and dropped his plate in the sink. Mkai fell into silence as Roger stared out the dirty window. Minutes dragged by as he waited patiently. Too much depended on Roger's help. Mkai was determined to give him the time and space he needed.

Roger finally turned from the window and slowly made his way back to his chair, carefully avoiding meeting Mkai's gaze. He took his time settling in his chair, fidgeting until he was comfortable.

With an almost inaudible sigh he looked up and met Mkai's gaze.

"We have kn-known each other a long time and in all that time I have called you f-friend. In my line of work, and with what I have gone through, I have learned to trust my instincts. I have very rarely been wrong in who I trust. I can't afford to make mistakes. B-But I must ask," he paused and Mkai could see the struggle in his friend, "are you evil?"

"No, my friend, I am not." Mkai said with a gentle smile as Roger visibly relaxed.

"I'm not evil. I have been on Earth to convert or corrupt Man but haven't sent a single soul to Hell. I've spent these years learning about Man, studying how you think, what you do. But that has all come to an end. There's no more time and I need your help."

Roger studied Mkai for a moment and then sat up and straightened his shoulders, "My h-help? Me? A feeble old man? H-how?"

25

"I found out something I wasn't supposed to know. I just came from a meeting with As'hame, one of the As'rai, an order of angels who came to earth to protect Man." Mkai said leaning towards him. "War is coming. War between angels and demons, and I need your help to stop it."

If the situation wasn't so critical Mkai would have burst out laughing at the look of alarm and confusion on Roger's face. As it was, it only evoked a small smile.

"I know it's a shock and I'm sorry," he said as Roger opened and closed his mouth several times. "I can give you more details later but it will have to wait; it's not safe for you to know too much. I have a lot to do and not a lot of time."

Roger held up a hand when Mkai opened his mouth to continue.

"You s-speak of Heaven and Hell, of angels and demons. I am sh-shocked, but not for the reasons you think. My parents lived through the G-Great War and they told me st-stories of miracles. Of faith. And of evil."

For the first time in their relationship, Mkai could see Roger's frustration with his stutter.

"I have seen things sc-science can't explain, and heard of more. You are my fr-friend. Th-that is enough for me."

The heartfelt honesty of the statement and the open, trusting gaze in Roger's eyes hit Mkai unexpectedly and he had to fight to keep his composure. It was so much more than he expected.

"Thank you, my friend. I can't tell you how much that means," Mkai said, catching Roger's eyes, willing him to understand exactly how deep his friendship touched him.

Mkai took a breath, "First, I have a list of equipment I need, some legal, some illegal. After that, I'll need some information, but for now it has to wait."

Mkai pulled a list from his jacket pocket and spread it on the low coffee table in front of him.

"I'll need weapons, a couple of handguns, shotguns, a couple of assault rifles and ammo for all of them. They're on the list. Radios or cell phones, clean and untraceable. A vehicle in good shape, probably an SUV. As new as you can get. There are other items, but these are most urgent," Mkai pushed the list across the table. "How soon do you think you can gather it all?"

Roger didn't reply as he studied the list, lips moving as he read. Mkai watched in silence as Roger leaned back and stared at the wall, tapping his front teeth with a finger in a long-familiar habit. Roger finally grinned. "I don't see a p-problem with the list. Give me th-three days and I'll have the SUV loaded with everything you n-need."

"Thank you. This means more than you will ever know." Mkai stood, reaching to shake Roger's hand. "For now, I must hurry. I will be back in three days. Be safe, my friend."

Mkai heard the door shut behind him and the locks snick back into place as he hurried down the hall and started down the stairs. With the equipment taken care of, he was now free to contact his network. He had people in virtually every large city around North America but it had been a while since he was last in Los Angeles and it was time to start up the network. Sam was the next closest.

He walked down the stairs, the echoes of his footsteps emphasizing the emptiness of the building. He went over the conversation with Roger in his head, still surprised at his acceptance. *The capacity humans have to love and trust is unbelievable sometimes. The truly are God's children.* Angels, and demons even, loved, but not in the way humans did. Humans slipped in and out of love, and there were degrees to it. *We have no choice, we love only God, and that's all we have.* Mkai let himself fully feel the love of God that was so much of every demon and angel. The heartache of loss almost drove him to his knees. Millennia of forced separation from the Light of Heaven hadn't lessened the love of God at the core of his existence. He forced the thought away with a struggle, sweat popping out on his forehead, tears threatening to fall. *No wonder we're all half crazy.*

Mkai stepped into the deserted street, the stench of the garbage strewn about almost overpowering. Compared to the noxious atmosphere of Hell it was nothing for him, but he didn't understand how the few people who stayed could stand it. With a glance up and down the street, he started walking north. It was several blocks until he'd be able to find a phone or hail a cab.

Within the hour, a cab dropped him off in front of yet another apartment. The street, still cluttered with trash, was cleaner than the one he just left with only light traffic this time of day. Mkai entered through the front, the slight security of a locked door long circumvented by the judicious use of a screwdriver and hammer. He made his way by the mailboxes, half missing their doors, and past the elevator. Roger's third floor apartment was a much easier climb than Sam's seventh floor.

Mkai decided to walk up instead of using the rickety elevator which had seen better days. Sam was only a regular contact. Mkai had never felt the same connection with him as he did with Roger, and honestly didn't trust him fully. He intended to give him the fewest instructions he would need to glean the information Mkai needed. Luckily Sam preferred as few details as possible.

The faint tang of blood caught Mkai's attention as he stepped out of the stairwell. He glanced up and down the hall, senses at full alert. He closed his eyes for a brief moment and let his subconscious float free, open to the sensations of the world around him. It exposed him and made him vulnerable, but he estimated the blood wasn't fresh and events had already played out. He felt several people in the building, but opening his eyes he felt sure he was the only non-human in the immediate area.

He strode down the hall, eyes searching and watching until he came to apartment 305. He put his ear against the door and stretched out his senses, focusing on any movement from the rooms within. Nothing. This time of day, Sam should still be home. It was far too early for him to be down at his bar, and home and the bar were the only two places he ever went. Sam was, for lack of a better description, a paranoid freak. He had hundreds of conspiracy theories, all of which Mkai had heard many times over the decades he'd known him.

Might as well get it over with.

With a hard shove he forced the door, the lock splintering with a harsh tearing sound, loud in the silence. The flood of blood scent and the scene of destruction hit him like a blow. Even with the millennia of experience behind him, the acts of barbarism, cruelty, and utter devastation he'd watched impassively over the years, what he saw hit him in the gut and he had to pause and take a deep breath. A corner of his mind marveled the neighbors hadn't raised an outcry even as he surveyed the room before him.

He stepped carefully through the carnage, working his way toward the body of the man he'd come to see. The odor of blood and burnt flesh overwhelmed him as he approached to stand above his contact. The man was barely recognizable as human. What skin hadn't been flayed was splattered with blood. Burns covered almost every part of the body he could see, some deep black craters while others covered by bubbled blisters. Sam's left arm was attached by strings of gristle and each finger broken and twisted. His right arm ended in hacked and raw stump; the missing hand appeared to have been torn or bitten off.

Mkai swallowed hard against the bile rising in his throat when he saw the charred space below the eviscerated and empty cavity of Sam's stomach. Beneath that horror, his legs had been broken in several places, stark white ragged bone driven through muscle. Mkai leaned closer and shuddered when he realized there were tooth marks on the edges of the bone. He stood up, shocked and disgusted, and looked at Sam's face, the only unmarred part of his body. The look of utter terror and pain on Sam's face stabbed into Mkai like a dagger in his heart. It screamed the fact Sam had been alive, and likely conscious, for most of the torture.

Mkai recognized who was responsible for the unspeakable acts visited upon Sam. The jagged teeth marks, the deep claw marks and the wanton destruction around him all pointed to one creature. Drekor. Drekor delighted in the torture of the living. She abhorred virtually everything on earth. Mkai had once watched her spend hours tearing into a grove, uprooting full grown trees, ripping up bushes, a storm of branches, leaves, and splinters filling the air. All because of a single birdsong. She delighted in death.

And she scares you a little bit; be honest with yourself. Mkai pulled a worn blanket free from the mangled remains of the couch. He remembered Sam wrapping himself in it against the cold as he railed against the wool monopoly and how they had controlled the world market for hundreds of years. Mkai smiled gently at the memory and carefully laid the woolen blanket over the remains before him.

"I'm sorry, Sam. Obviously word has got out about me and you are one of my known contacts." Mkai murmured sadly, looking around him. "They were looking for information about me but you wouldn't have known anything. It's been seven years since we spoke last. I'm sorry."

He walked out of the apartment, pulling the door closed behind him. There wasn't anything he could do for Sam, but if he hurried, perhaps he could still reel in the rest of his net before it was too late. With that thought, he rushed down the stairs, taking them two and even three at a time. He burst out onto the street and, with a glimmer of luck, hailed a cab. Sirens in the distance told him perhaps the neighbors had noticed more than he thought.

"MacArthur Park, as fast as you can," he told the cab driver, slamming the door.

The cabbie jerked at Mkai's barked command and he slammed the car into gear, tires squealing as they darted into the road.

CHAPTER FIVE

Paul stepped out onto the street and paused. He put his hands on the small of his back and leaning backwards, stretched until he felt his spine creak. Rolling his shoulders, he worked a kink out of his neck. He made fists with his hands, squeezing and relaxing, wiggling his fingers to get the stiffness out. His hands always ached after a long shift and last night had been a long one. One of the few benefits to working the night shift at UPS was having so much of the day to enjoy.

He yawned and looked around. This early, there were few people on the street but it would start picking up soon as more people made their way to work. Paul squinted against the sun, barely up but promising a hot day. Loading delivery trucks all night was hard work sometimes, monotonous at others, but, on mornings like this, it was totally worth it. The anticipation of a sunny day fresh from the night's rain, and the freedom to do anything he liked elicited a smile. A few white clouds floated high in the sky against a blue so clear it almost hurt to look at it. Yes, days this spectacular made the long nights worth it.

He slipped on his sunglasses, tucking the ear pieces under his shaggy black hair. *Time for a haircut.* Grinning to himself, he strolled down the street, content being one of the few in L.A. not totally focused on his appearance. Everyone else walked with purpose, focused on their destination, with the inward gaze of the self-involved. They were at odds with his unhurried gait, that of someone with a place to be but no hurry to get there. He nodded at the occasional pedestrian he passed, not bothered by the weird looks he'd get sometimes. He was pretty used to that after years of living in L.A.

Paul breathed deep as he wandered down the street. Underneath the ever-present smog filling the air, he tasted the freshness from the rain the night before. It rained on and off for most of the week but today looked like a day to enjoy. The few clouds in the sky soaring fluffy and white against the blue, perfect for lying on a hill and watching, laughing with a lover over the shapes they made.

At that thought, his mood soured abruptly. He used to have someone with whom he could share a beautiful day. But no more. *That was months ago; you're over it.* His sudden laugh made a couple walking by him start in surprise. Very little concern though, this was L.A. after all. People laughing to themselves, or having complete conversations with themselves was not unusual. He could tell himself all he wanted that he was over Laura leaving, but that didn't make it true. Though at least he could laugh about it now. *I'll be okay. Laughing is the first step.*

Paul's thoughts drifted back over the past three years as he strolled down the sidewalk. Up until the day he arrived home eight months ago, he thought their relationship was solid. He and Laura had their typical problems, as any long-term relationship did, but nothing major. Mostly the small irritants of two people with their own way of doing things sharing a space. *And they really were small irritants. At least, for me.* But until he opened the door to a half-empty apartment, he thought they were okay. The last thing he expected was her to leave without warning. The note she left for him on the worn kitchen counter told him how wrong he was. He carefully unfolded it, echoes of heartbreak filling the air as he read.

Paul didn't think he would ever forget the image of the note, the black ink stark against the pink stationery.

> *I'm sorry Paul, but I can't live this lie any longer. I tried. I tried so hard and for so long. But I can't fool myself anymore. You are a great guy, you really are. So kind, so thoughtful and sweet to me. A part of me, a large part of me, says this is a mistake. But you have . . . something missing. There's a hollow inside you, this emptiness I could never reach. Since we first met, there's been a feeling of waiting, like the world is a moment from revealing itself. That part of you I couldn't touch, something inside you, always keeping me at arm's length. I love you Paul, you fill my heart and make me sing like no one I've ever met. But the smiles were always twinned with hidden tears. So I'm letting you go. I'm taking steps to make my life the one it's meant to be. Your life is waiting for you; I know you can feel it. But I have to leave to find mine. I'm sorry to do this to you, and in a note. But I just couldn't do it in person. I'm not strong enough to face you. Please don't look for me.*
>
> *Love, Laura*

The last part of the note was scrawled in a hurry, tracks and spots of tears covering the page. His heart ached even now remembering it. He never imagined she had been so unhappy. Laura helped keep the loneliness at bay for the years they'd been together and a part of him truly did love her. But, being honest with himself, Paul knew and understood what she meant. He was aware of the hollow inside him, the feeling of the world waiting on him, as if there was some big thing he was meant to do. He knew firsthand how difficult it was to live with it. How it influenced his behavior and how he interacted with people. And that feeling had been getting stronger in the last year.

The world felt like it was holding its breath, waiting on him to *do* something. It had always been there: a silence in his soul that kept getting louder and louder. And it was getting more and more frustrating. Every morning he woke up and the first thing he was aware of, even before he noticed whether the sun was up or not, was that silence, the sense of the world pausing, expecting something from him. *And you have absolutely no idea what.* He shook off the feeling, letting the frustration and anger go, knowing, if he didn't, he'd lose the entire day mulling it over. And not for the first time.

He stopped on a corner, faced with a dilemma, a choice. Turn right and return to an apartment that still felt empty. Or walk straight toward Elysian Park and Dodger stadium. He didn't care much for baseball but the park felt like home. He rarely went up to the stadium itself, spending most of his time in the park, wandering the paths or sitting and watching the fountain and the people. It felt like a second home to him.

Just that simple: the park it was. Not that there was really a question. There was very little waiting for him at home. *She even took the ficus.* That thought brought another laugh and Paul continued down the street, lost in thought.

"Careful!"

The yell just behind him jerked him from his daze. The hand grabbing him and yanking him backwards still startled him enough he staggered and would have fallen except for the solid grip on his arm. The Mustang flying through the intersection snapped him completely out of his reverie. It must have been doing at least seventy, with three LAPD units right behind it as it sped through the intersection. Only then did he realize he had been hearing the sirens without paying attention.

He watched, still in shock at the close call, as the car careened out of control. It tried to make a corner two blocks up but lost control, sliding across the intersection, almost flipping before slamming into several parked cars. He pulled his gaze from the wreckage and turned to his savior where she stood beside him.

"Thank you hardly seems enough for saving my life."

"You were pretty lost in thought there. What was I supposed to do, let you be turned into a hood ornament?" she said, the tiniest smile crinkling the corner of her mouth.

Paul smiled back as he looked at his rescuer. At five and a half feet tall she still had a waifish air to her, though the way she pulled him from the street spoke of strength hidden from view. She wore a pair of blue jeans, form-fitting but not ultra-tight, tucked into a pair of worn biker boots. A short, dark brown leather jacket topped a deep blue blouse with the sheen of silk. The narrow v-neck showed just the hint of tanned cleavage. Paul noted those details, even the cleavage, only in passing, unable to tear his gaze away from her eyes.

Her light grey eyes, flecked with gold and old sorrow, utterly captivated him. The slightest of lines around her eyes told him she didn't laugh often, but when she did, it was with her whole face. A part of him really wanted to see her face light up in a laugh. Her long, dark hair was parted just off center and fell in waves, framing high cheekbones with a slight dusting of freckles on her nose. *She is gorgeous.* One side of her mouth tilted and, with a start, he realized he was staring.

"I don't think I'd work as a replacement for the mustang on the hood, so it would have indeed been a waste," he said, a blush threatening to burst forth. "My name is Paul."

"Hello Paul," she said, the freckles on her nose catching the sun. "You be more careful now"

"Wait!" He surprised himself by calling after her as she turned to walk away. "I was heading to the park to enjoy the morning. Let me buy you a coffee as a thank you," he said, not wanting her to disappear.

She turned back to him, a guarded look appearing on her face. Paul heard a faint siren, an ambulance he guessed, as he waited for her to respond. He didn't understand why but he was anxious she not walk away from him. "Please."

"Is that what your life is worth to you? A coffee?" she finally said, sweeping her long dark hair over her left ear.

"Well, it's worth considerably more than that," he said, grinning, "But until I get paid, or win the lottery, it'll have to do."

That brought a smile, which lit her face, and Paul felt his heart skip a little.

Relief flooded him as she shrugged. "Okay, what did you have in mind?"

"Coffee, or tea if you prefer."

"Coffee will do."

"Is there a spot in particular you like?" he said as the light turned.

"Nope, you're paying so doesn't matter to me, as long as it's not Starbucks."

"You're not a Starbucks fan either?"

He received a small grin for that.

"How about Cafe de Camacho on Main?"

"Sounds fine."

"Okay, let's go."

Another small grin and, after looking both ways, she started across the street, which moments ago would have been his death if not for her.

"Wait, what's your name?" he asked before she got too far ahead.

"Call me Rie," she said, "everyone else does."

"Rie? That's unique, what does it mean?"

"Nothing special. It's short for Marie."

He looked after her for a couple steps, not sure why, but he knew he just turned a corner in his life. The feeling of the world waiting became stronger as Rie walked away. *There is something going on here.* Good or bad, he didn't know yet, but he'd learned a long time ago not to question or try to decipher those unknown feelings. He quickly checked both ways before following her, curious to see what destiny had in store for him.

CHAPTER SIX

They walked in silence for a moment or two and then Paul spoke.

"So I just got off work. I work the night shift at UPS."

She looked at him and raised an eyebrow. "Oh, and you're telling me this because . . ."

"Well I figured maybe you should know about the life you saved." A full smile this time.

"Then by all means, continue. We have a couple of blocks to go so I'm a captive audience. For now."

Paul couldn't help but grin back at her over the taunt. He took a moment, thinking about what else to say, while sneaking looks at her. *She really fills out those jeans well.* He pulled his eyes away with difficulty.

"Like I said, I work nights at UPS. It sounds crazy but I really enjoy my job. It's not difficult, but it can be taxing at times. Both physically and mentally."

He paused to give her a chance to say something and when she didn't he continued.

"I work the night shift because I'm a night guy and I don't really sleep much. And having most of the day to enjoy doesn't hurt either."

She looked at him for a moment. "So you were headed home, then?"

"No, not exactly," he started and then paused.

There was an appraising look in her eyes as she waited for him to continue.

"I was heading to Elysian Park, not really in the mood to go home."

"Oh?"

He took a breath. Paul surprised himself by blurting out, "Eight months ago my girlfriend moved out, left me a note and an empty apartment"

He looked at her and shrugged, "I'm still not used to it yet so I decided to go for a walk first."

Rie seemed to take his personal confession in stride, although Paul wondered what on earth possessed him to say such a thing to a perfect stranger. One who had saved his life, true, but still . . .

"A note? That seems rather harsh."

"I don't think she meant it that way," unable to stop the sorrow filling his voice. "She said she was sorry for doing it that way but she couldn't face doing it in person."

"You must have meant a lot to her if she couldn't bear to face you." she said, her head tilting slightly as she studied him.

"I never looked at it that way. I just figured she was scared or something. Thank you. That actually makes it hurt less."

Rie shrugged.

"So yeah, I'm still not completely used to the silence. One of the drawbacks to being up during the day. I go to the park a couple times a week. I love it there." Paul felt like he was babbling, but he also felt something about this girl was special. He couldn't seem to hold anything back.

"The people watching," she said.

"Yes! Exactly!" he said, happy she understood, "I love sitting and watching people. The news is always so negative but sitting in the park and watching all the happy couples and families together gives me hope."

"That's kind of why I do it, too. Even if it hurts at times."

He didn't think he was supposed to hear the last whispered part and, after a moment, he awkwardly continued.

"I've been in L.A. for years, came out here just a bit after high school. The city is full of craziness but I love it all the same. There is such a huge range of people here, it's never boring."

"It never is."

Paul smiled slightly at her, not sure how to take her comment. He felt an undercurrent of . . . something, but he couldn't quite decide what it was. Bitterness?

"Cafe de Camacho is just up ahead," he said, pointing up ahead at the obvious billboard sitting on the sidewalk.

"Okay."

Nice, you sound like a babbling idiot.

He reached to open the door for her but she beat him to it and, with a quick glance, she opened it and he followed her in. The line to order wasn't long and several tables stood empty. Rie stepped up to the end of the line and started looking over the menu. Paul stood quietly beside her.

"Is the coffee good here?"

For some reason her question caught him off-guard. "It's quite good actually. They have a really amazing Mexican blend. The fact you don't like Starbucks bodes well for your taste in coffee, so I think you'll enjoy anything here."

She looked at him and then back to the menu.

"The sandwiches are pretty good but their muffins are great."

She nodded as the line moved. *She doesn't really have much to say but not in a 'leave me alone' way.* He couldn't help but admit that he found it rather intriguing. On one side she seemed rather aloof and closed but when she'd look at him and smile, he saw a totally different side. *She's obviously guarded but seems open at the same time.*

The background babble of the typical coffee house emphasized the silence between them, but somehow it didn't make Paul uncomfortable. He was satisfied with letting things develop, without pushing. It was something he was struggling to learn, especially after Laura. After she left, his coworkers expressed concern because Paul changed from being chatty to uncommunicative. He had given up trying to explain to his friends that, lately, he just didn't feel like talking. *In truth, you gave too much of yourself away, opened yourself up too much and too soon.* A trace of sadness crossed his heart. The way he had just opened up to Rie was the first time he'd spoken of anything emotionally close in months, and he still couldn't figure out why.

He looked at the menu board without really seeing it until he became aware of Rie staring at him. He met her eyes for a moment, the understanding in them surprising him. A half-smile formed on her lips and he felt a burden lift even as she turned to the barista.

"I'll have a cup of coffee, Mexican blend, black, and a piece of the lemon poppy seed."

"Sure thing, and the usual?" the smiling barista asked, looking at Paul.

"Hey! Where's my coffee?" a large burly man said, pushing between Paul and Rie.

"It's being made sir," the barista said.

"It shouldn't take this long," the man said, anger rising in his voice.

"If you look, you can see it's being made right now," Paul interrupted, drawing the man's eyes as he pointed. "If you wait but a couple moments more it will be ready."

The man met Paul's gaze for a moment or two, anger slowly draining away, before turning to the barista. "I'm sorry for being rude."

The man nodded to Paul and walked to the other counter, standing patiently for his order. Paul looked at Marie with a shrug and then turned to the barista.

"Sorry about that, Lisa. Not the usual today, I'll have a cafe latte and a chocolate chip muffin." Paul smiled. "I'll get it all."

"Thank you for that. That'll be ten dollars with the hero discount," she smiled.

He grinned and passed over a ten and collected the muffin and the cake. He passed the lemon poppy seed to Rie and followed her to a corner table. She slid out a chair, and unzipping her jacket, sat down. He pulled the other chair out and sat facing her. They looked at each other in silence for a moment and he felt the flush wanting to rush to his cheeks.

"Napkins. I'll get napkins," he blurted.

She broke off a small piece of cake and popped it into her mouth with a grin, "Thank you."

He walked to the counter shaking his head. *Come on man, what the hell is wrong with you? She isn't the first pretty woman you've ever talked to. Get your shit together.* He picked up a handful of napkins and turned back to the table when their order was called. He caught Rie's eye and motioned to her to stay seated. She settled back into her chair with a nod and Paul stepped to the counter.

"Thanks, Lisa," he said, gathering the coffee.

"You're welcome, Paul. She's pretty."

"Sorry, what?" Paul asked in confusion.

"Your girl, silly. She's pretty."

Paul looked at Rie and back to Lisa. "She is, but she's not my girl." He lifted one cup in a silent "cheers" and walked toward the table. "Here's your coffee," he said, setting both cups on the table and settling in his chair.

"Thank you."

"The least I can do." Paul said breaking off a piece of his muffin. "I see you liked the poppy seed."

She popped the last piece in her mouth and nodded, "Yep, it hit the spot."

There was a frank look in her eyes that Paul didn't quite know how to deal with so he busied himself breaking apart his muffin.

"Do you know Lisa well?"

The question confused him and he looked at the counter quickly and then back to Rie. "Lisa? Not really, I've been coming here a couple times a week for several years so I know her a little bit."

The wry look on Rie's face and the way she tilted her head did nothing to ease his confusion.

"You don't see it, do you?"

"See what?" Paul asked.

"Lisa. She likes you. And she's not all that happy to see me here, with you."

"What? You're totally wrong. She's just nice to me because it's her job."

"I'm a bartender and waitress. I can recognize 'being nice because of the job' and that's not it. She likes you."

Paul shook his head. "I think you're wrong. Besides, I don't see her that way."

The only answer Rie had to that was a raised eyebrow as she took a sip from her mug.

"Mmm, you're right, it is good coffee."

Paul, relieved at the change of subject, took too large a gulp of his latte.

"Ow!"

He set his coffee down quickly, his scalded tongue making his eyes water.

"Hot?"

Her innocent question, asked beneath eyes sparkling with humor made him laugh and unexpectedly he felt something spark to life in his chest. Her eyes, when lit with humor as they were now, spoke to something in Paul, something which had never been touched before. He fought to hide it even as he felt it stretch out to her.

"Um, not at all, quite cool actually." he said, words only slightly skewed because of his tender tongue.

She grinned back at him and took another careful sip.

"Does that kind of thing happen often?" she asked.

"Does what happen?" Paul asked confused.

"That man, the one who got angry about his coffee. You calmed him down with a couple words. It seemed very natural to you so I wondered if it happened often?"

"Oh that." Paul smiled, thinking about her question for a moment. "I guess it does happen sometimes. I don't like to see people fight and argue over stupid things and I can't seem to help stepping in and stopping it if I can."

He met her even gaze for a moment before lowering his eyes to the muffin in front of him. He took another bite and picked up his cup. The heat warmed his hands, almost too hot to hold.

"So, I don't know anything about you, besides your name. What else should I know about my rescuer?"

Rie went still and the look on her face was so hard that for a moment Paul thought he had made a huge mistake.

"I'm sorry, I don't mean to impose, or push; I'm just curious." Paul said, "You don't have to answer."

He saw her weighing things in her mind. Paul waited, hoping to learn more about her, but feeling if he pushed too hard he would get nothing. And for some reason, he felt this woman was someone very important to him, even though they had just met. His world teetered beneath his feet, balanced, waiting for her response.

"That's all right; nothing says you can't ask questions."

Her reply brought a sigh of relief from Paul. He leaned forward as she continued.

"As I said, my name is Marie, though most people call me Rie. I work nights as a bartender in a local bar. I do it for some of the same reasons you work at night. It gives me the day to do things. I'm also a night person. And I'm quite good at my job."

"I can see that. Every female bartender I've ever seen has been attractive."

She raised an eyebrow and he realized what he'd said.

"I'm sorry, I didn't meant to say you couldn't get any other job or that you only got your job because of your looks." Paul felt the heat in his cheeks and wondered how red his face had become.

"Oh? So are you saying I'm not attractive enough to be a bartender?"

"No! That's not what I meant at all!" he said, feeling more and more flustered.

"Don't worry, Paul, I'm only teasing," Rie said, laughing.

Paul felt a shiver run through him at her use of his name. He smiled and shook his head at her. "You're very good at making me feel silly and off balance."

"I'm sorry; it's a reflex, a habit, for me sometimes. I don't mean anything by it."

The honest, focused look on her face verified the truth of her statement and he found himself waving her apology away.

"Oh no, don't apologize. Don't worry about it. I don't mind being teased." He paused and grinned, "Especially by someone as beautiful as you."

It was his turn to watch her blush at his compliment; he grinned again and took a large swallow of his latte, now blessedly cool enough not to burn.

CHAPTER SEVEN

Rie felt the blush hit her cheeks, quite unexpectedly. She was used to fending off compliments; as a bartender, she got them every night. But those were mostly from drunks, and it was usually dark. And she was working so it was easy to shrug them off. To have this charming and handsome man tell her she was beautiful—it was difficult for her to process. It threw her off balance. She was not used to being off balance, to not feeling in control. The blush still felt like a betrayal though, even as she rationalized it. *Calm down girl, you can deal with compliments better than this!*

"So, if your girlfriend left eight months ago, and obviously the barrista likes you, why are you still single?" she said, and then could have hidden under the table at her stupidity.

From the look of shock on his face, she worried she had gone too far.

"I'm sorry, that came out rather abrupt and rude." she quickly apologized, "You don't have to answer."

She watched Paul set down his coffee, twisting the cup around slowly, his shaggy dark hair falling across his forehead and ears. She wanted to run her hands through it, not something she ever remembered thinking about anyone, ever. The hair and his day-old scruff made him look a little dangerous but that impression disappeared as he looked up at her and grinned.

"No, that's okay, it wasn't rude. It's part of getting to know each other," he said. "And I do find myself wanting to get to know you. But it does go both ways, you're going to have to tell me stuff, too."

"Deal."

Relief she hadn't offended him warred with nerves. She was never comfortable with telling people details of her life, especially strangers. Regardless of the connection she felt with Paul, it wasn't something easy for her.

"Good. Then it's your turn." Paul's grin made it difficult for her to keep her stoic expression. In fact, she was having a difficult time keeping a straight face. She had always prided herself in staying detached and reserved, keeping everyone at arm's length. For some reason, she was having a hard time doing that with Paul.

"You know my name. And what I do for a living. What else is there?" she equivocated.

Paul just grinned and raised an eyebrow.

"I work at a place called Naco's. I've been there for about seven years. I am single as well. Mostly because with my job and the bar, it's almost impossible to find even a half-decent guy." She paused and took a breath, "And frankly I like being alone. It's easier."

"I can understand that."

She smiled. "And like you, I often spend my days wandering around people watching."

"What about family?"

The innocent question set alarm bells ringing she tried hard to ignore. "I'm an only child."

She saw him absorb that, as well as the abruptness she couldn't help in her reply. Rie was surprised at what Paul said next.

"I'm an only child as well. Or at least as far as I know."

She quirked her head, confused by his comment.

"I'm adopted. My adopted parents didn't have any other children. So as far as I know, I'm an only child," he said.

Rie marveled at the ease at which he dropped the rather personal information. "I'm sorry, it's my turn to apologize again. I didn't mean to pry."

"Oh no, it's okay. You didn't pry, I volunteered. Besides, I asked about family first. And I'm quite all right with it. I was adopted quite young. I barely remember anything before them and they were great parents to me."

"Were?" she asked, the words slipping out unbidden.

The quiet question hit him hard she could see, and he took a slow sip of his latte before responding. "Yes. They passed away ten years ago, just after I graduated high school."

"I'm very sorry. I can imagine how it must have felt." Rie suppressed a pang, and wondered at the similarities of their experiences. *This is getting a little weird, but not in a bad way.*

"Your parents passed too?"

"My mom passed away when I was fifteen. I've been on my own ever since." Rie couldn't believe what she was saying. Only the other bartender, Tony, knew this much about her; and it had taken three years, and rather a lot of whiskey one night for her to share. *What is it about this guy?*

"Your mom. So no dad?"

She expected the question so answered it easily. "Nope. He left before my first birthday and never heard anything from him after that."

"I'm sorry?"

She caught the question in his tone, as well as the understanding look in his eyes.

"Oh, that's okay, I've never felt the lack of a father and, like you said, I'm quite all right with it."

Not that he would have made a difference anyway. The thought came unbidden to her, but it was a truth she had long accepted.

Having a father in the picture likely wouldn't have made that big of a difference in her childhood, and less than that in how she turned out.

Paul's expression spoke of an eerie level of understanding, almost like he could read her mind. His level gaze meeting hers touched her, touched her in an unfamiliar, but not uncomfortable, way. She fought the slight shiver running down her spine and tried to think of something to change the subject.

"Your turn now. What else should I know about who I rescued? Why did your girlfriend break up with you? How long were you together?"

"We were together almost three years, lived together for two," he said, sitting back in his chair. "And why did she break up with me? Well, according to her note, there is an emptiness inside me she couldn't touch. And she couldn't take it anymore."

Rie watched Paul glance out the window. There was vulnerability in him at this moment she didn't expect. He might be flippant about the whole thing but it was obvious, at least to her, the experience had hurt him deeply. Not just because his girlfriend left, but because she blamed him so bluntly as well. *And that is a rather harsh thing to say to someone, especially through a note.* Rie wasn't too impressed with the image of the woman forming in her mind.

She repeated her thoughts aloud. "That's rather harsh, especially in a note. Do you think she was right?"

"Well, I guess I understand what she meant and why she did it that way, in a note. And she was kind of right in a way, about the emptiness," he said. "But it's more waiting on something than being empty. Know what I mean?"

"I know exactly what you mean." she said, and oddly enough, she did.

"It's like the world's waiting on me to do something. Waiting for me to figure it out. There's something I was meant to do, I just don't know what. Like, it's behind a closed door and I don't know how to open it. It's always been there, but lately it seems it's started to knock on the door trying to make itself known."

"What happens if you never open the door, never find what you're 'meant to do'?" she quietly asked.

"I . . . I honestly don't know," Paul said. He looked down at his hands. "I've never thought about it much. I try not to think about the feeling. It's just always been there, in the back of my mind. I've never considered what it would be like to never find what it means."

"I know what you're talking about, at least a little. I've never thought of it quite that way though," Rie said, pushing away her coffee with a small sigh. *In for a dime . . .*

"I know I had potential for a different life; I was meant to do, to be, something different . . . but sometimes life doesn't work out that way. Sometimes you've lived one life too long to change." She spoke the last softly, and was relieved when Paul didn't react to it.

They looked at each other for a moment, silently, the hum of conversation a gentle background to their thoughts. She felt a connection with Paul that was something new for her. It was obvious to her Paul felt it, too. No matter how strange the circumstances, Rie knew there was something special about this man.

Rie took a deep breath. "I think we have some of the same issues, or at least similar ones," she continued. "I've done things, made choices, because I've been trying to find my role in life. I haven't had any luck," she said. "But maybe together we can help each other."

"You think so?" he asked.

"I think I happened to be on that street, at just the right moment to save you. I was there for a reason, and I think it may be because we were supposed to meet."

"Hmm. Say that we were supposed to meet, what's next?"

"We finish our coffee?" she said.

They both laughed and relaxed, sitting back in their chairs.

"Are you in a hurry or would you like another cup?"

"I have time, and would love a second cup."

Paul nodded as he rose, "I'll be right back."

She watched as he walked to the counter, appreciating the view. Blue jeans over work boots with a black leather jacket enhanced his dangerous air, at least until he smiled. His strong shoulders tapered down to a narrow waist and his strong, confident walk definitely drew eyes. *And he's got a nice butt.* Rie felt a slight pang of jealousy and fought to ignore it when the barista leaned over the counter as Paul approached.

It is more than the nice butt though, it's in his eyes. They're kind, like I could tell him anything and he'd never judge. Like he'd never hurt me. Rie shook her head and told herself to stop being so silly. She kept telling herself to not rush things, to let them develop, knowing it was a futile effort. Rie knew she could tell herself anything she wanted, but if she was going to fall there was nothing she could do about it.

"Did you have plans for today?" he asked as he returned with their refills.

"Not really, I usually spend the mornings doing errands and sleep in the afternoon before heading to work," she said. "Why?"

"I was thinking you're right. Saving my life is worth more than a coffee. I thought if you didn't have plans we could walk around a bit, maybe go to the park, and I could buy you lunch."

Rie picked up her coffee and studied Paul for a moment. While she relished the thought of spending more of the day with him, to her surprise, she wasn't sure if she was ready for it. Spending several more hours together would definitely make it much harder for her to keep her normal distance. *It's already been a strange day, how much weirder can it get?* She nodded and drank the last of her coffee.

"I would like that."

CHAPTER EIGHT

Memory can be both a blessing and a curse. Remembering the feel of the wind or the rush of air from the first time riding a bike. The tender, shy touch of a first kiss; these are happy memories bringing a smile in the face of loneliness. The heartache and confusion felt as a child at the loss of a loved one or the flush of humiliation and embarrassment of building up the courage to ask for a dance, seeing the look of scorn and hearing a dismissive "No." Memory can bring sweet joy or crushing heartache.

Of all the unique gifts given to the different classes and ranks of angels, one of the most exquisite was perfect memory. Every sight, every smell, and every sound was captured for all time. This gift was one of only a handful shared among every class; every angel, ranked high or low, possessed this gift, one of the very few left to the fallen. Not only could Mkai remember every turn of every path he'd ever walked, every face of every person he'd ever met, but also every note of every song of Heaven.

Being cast out of Heaven was pain enough to crush the strongest in waves of despair. The ache of loss increased immeasurably with each moment since; the crystal clear memory of what was lost a taint touching everything. Mkai privately thought the constant ache filling the days since Heaven was barred from them was part of what made some of his brethren so cruel and vicious. It seemed the more powerful ones, those who had been the most honored, the most blessed by His presence in Heaven, experienced the most excruciating fall. God was beyond pettiness but He did have His own view of punishment and leaving the fallen with perfect memory was indeed just that—punishment.

At this moment, Mkai was thankful for the gift of perfect memory. As he moved quickly through the increasing traffic of joggers, people hurrying home from work, and those just out for a stroll, he easily retraced the steps of the first time he had walked this path. The mid-afternoon sun sent his shadow out before him as he walked. His mind worked through more important things, his steps instinctive even after so many years.

He traced back to the first time he had met his next contact and how even he, after hundreds of years mingling with the refuse of mankind, was surprised how resourceful such a young girl could be. Only eighteen then, she had an edge to her and, he learned with a few discreet questions, she was no easy mark. A group of men discovered this for themselves. Of those who accosted her, one was sent to the morgue and three to the hospital. After that, she was left alone and treated with a wary respect.

Like his other contacts, she was a collector. While some gathered things, what she collected for Mkai was information. He felt a pang for Sam. He would have preferred to use Sam for this and keep Marie out of it, but he had no choice. As a bartender in a rather seedy bar, she had a keen eye for detail and a knack for getting information his other contacts couldn't.

The way she delivered it, flavored with her sardonic wit, revealed more of her nature than she realized and it all combined to make Marie one of his favorites. It was because of this Mkai hurried faster than usual, distracted with worry about what he might find. He'd always been most careful in dealings with her, the same as with Roger, hoping his precautions had served to keep her safe. Mkai ached at the thought of Marie suffering the same fate as Sam.

This distraction almost got him killed.

He had just taken a right into an alley and started to jog, lost in thought, when he finally realized the danger. He dove to the right, narrowly missing a pile of garbage, and rolled back up to his feet, drawing his dagger. A sword blade slid a hair's breadth from his head and dug a small chunk from the brick wall of the alley. His dive had barely taken him under the blade and the clang of metal on the brick still lingered in the air as he rolled to his feet and stood waiting.

"Almost, Mkai," Rahale said, stepping from the shadows. "Where are you rushing off to? Another contact perhaps? Have we missed one?"

The last question was asked with an evil sneer and Mkai's heart plummeted, thinking of his other contacts around the city.

"No matter, if we missed one or two we'll find them. Then Drekor can feast again."

"You're back to fight? What makes you think you will fare better this time?"

"What makes you think I came on my own?"

Rahale's grin grew bigger, showing a mouth full of sharp teeth as two forms stepped from the shadows. Mkai shifted his feet. *Fight or flight.* He tightened his grip on his dagger when he recognized who stood before him. If he had an enemy, it was Ortag. Their rivalry had turned bitter and the only thing keeping one from giving the other the final death blow was Samael's rule against death challenges. From the gleam in Ortag's single eye, Kalia had obviously lifted that restriction. Flight might not be an option any longer.

Gaptoz, Ortag's companion, bulked large and threatening on the other side of Rahale, and even Ortag seemed to have a hard time controlling him. He was second in his lust for blood and terror only to Drekor and looked positively excited for the fight to come. His large hands kept opening and closing, claws drawing blood when he squeezed too hard. Gaptoz absently lifted his hands and licked the blood from his fingers.

"It's finally over Mkai, after so very long. I knew this day would eventually come," Ortag snarled, drawing his own sword. "I have ached for the day when I could drink your life's blood."

Gaptoz pulled a huge club from over his shoulder with a grunt and grinned, fangs dripping.

"This won't be quick," Rahale said, stepping forward.

Mkai said nothing in reply, refusing to be drawn in by their taunts. He spread his legs and readied himself for the attack, regret tight in his chest.

I'm sorry, As'hame. I won't be able to aid you in your quest.

With a snarl, Gaptoz leapt at Mkai, swinging his club hard enough to fell a tree. Mkai easily rolled under the wild swing, the whistling club ruffling his hair as it flew by. He slashed at Gaptoz's thick calf, blood spurting free drawing a snarl from Gaptoz as he lumbered by. Mkai rolled up and stood, no time for a thrust to a kidney or a hamstring cut. He parried a killing thrust from Rahale, using the momentum to twist Rahale, spinning him in time to dodge the hard overhead blow from Ortag. In their eagerness to be the first to draw blood, the three stepped in each other's way, the only thing giving Mkai hope to survive. Fighting any one of them singly would have been a battle. With all three at once, Mkai didn't harbor many hopes of walking away. He hardened his resolve and swore to take at least one of them with him.

"I can't believe the three of you are the best Hell has to send after me," he taunted. "A crooked sneak, a one-eyed deviant, and a slack-wit thug. Hell must really have no further use for you to send you to your deaths."

"You are delusional, Mkai," Ortag said. "All of Hell would clamor for the chance to come after you. Kalia will reward us well for this. Any one of us would be enough, but all three of us have equal claims to your death."

"You should have brought more. Do you not remember who you're dealing with, Ortag? Did your intelligence leak out along with your eye? I am Mkai, and I am never alone when I have this."

He drew the Ar'kt dagger and, with a feral grin, held it up for them to see. He saw the sudden fear at the sight of the specialized dagger, forged for one purpose only—to tear the life from otherworldly creatures. Most weapons like it had been lost through the shadows of time.

He saw his enemies start to weigh options and he knew the only hope he had of surviving even moments longer was to cloud their reason with rage. Thankfully, that was something easily done with the three before him. Demons were never far from rage and these three were closer most.

"Come, Ortag, and I'll take the other eye before I gut you like a pig," he taunted. Mkai took pleasure in the perfect memory of the stroke that laid open Ortag's face and destroyed his eye. That battle had taken place in Hell's domain and, unlike wounds taken on the earthen plane, there was no healing. He saw the fire rage in Ortag's remaining eye as the curse of perfect memory reminded the demon of that earlier battle.

With a shout, he charged at Mkai, sword rising high for a colossal blow. Instead of dodging to the side, Mkai leaped to intercept the blow, his first dagger sliding through the offense. Ortag screamed as the Ar'kt blade sliced across his ribs, a desperate twist saving him from the disemboweling cut. He stumbled forward holding his ribs, Mkai momentarily forgotten. Mkai slid sideways in an attempt to keep from facing the other two at once. Rahale approached carefully, Gaptoz following close behind, a slight limp the only sign of the slice to his calf.

From the guarded expression on his face, Mkai knew he wouldn't be able to enrage Rahale so easily. But he had other options.

"Come, Gaptoz, that little cut can't have hurt that bad." he snarled, carefully keeping Rahale between them. "You have fallen far if you've taken to hiding behind the skirts of one like this."

He smiled at the roar of anger as Gaptoz shook his club and bellowed.

"Is that the real reason you've preyed upon humans for so long? You've grown weak, timid, and afraid to face a real fight."

"Enough, Gaptoz! Ignore the traitor! We're here to execute him," Rahale growled.

"Listen to your master howl with the sear of the Ar'kt blade, Gaptoz. Know you only feel the cut of an ordinary blade. Run in fear of the Ar'kt bite and leave him to his fate, you cur!" Mkai shouted.

The yell of outrage startled even Mkai and broke Rahale's concentration enough for him to turn and glance behind him. This was the chance Mkai needed. He leaped forward. Rahale turned back and swung wildly against a stroke Mkai never made. Instead of striking with the dagger, Mkai rammed forward with his shoulder, shoving Rahale toward Gaptoz. This enraged the giant even more and he swung his club, knocking Rahale into the side of the building.

That's two out for a couple minutes. You have to finish this oaf quick.

He knew it wouldn't be an easy job. Gaptoz was a brute and much faster than he should have been. Mkai had to keep him enraged.

"Now what are you going to do? You have no one to hide behind," Mkai laughed.

Gaptoz just bellowed again and swung his club. His reptilian eyes watched, gauging Mkai's movements. Mkai saw Rahale struggle to his hands and knees, shaking his head, trying to clear it to stand. From the moans of pain behind him, Mkai knew Ortag was still out of it as well.

"Here, little one, I'll put away my big scary dagger. Surely, you can't be afraid of just one," Mkai said, taking a chance and sliding the Ar'kt blade back in its sheath and beckoning with the empty hand.

Mkai watched the giant's eyes glaze over with rage and grinned. His joy was short lived as, with a bellow, Gaptoz charged, club swinging. Mkai did the only thing he could. He ran. He turned and bolted straight back down the alley, Gaptoz right on his heels. Mkai tore down the alley, eyes roaming. He felt the rush of the club as Gaptoz swung, screams of rage echoing all around them.

He finally saw what he wanted and changed course slightly. With a scream Mkai leaped forward and sprung off the dumpster lid toward the wall, feet first. He bent his legs, taking up the shock and then, shoving hard, twisted his body. He arced up, drawing the Ar'kt dagger as he twisted, Gaptoz's charge taking him into the dumpster.

With a cry of triumph he leaped forward, Ar'kt dagger leading the way. Gaptoz straightened, mouth open wide in a shriek as first one then the other dagger found his kidneys. The pain of his mortal wounds drove Gaptoz first to his toes and then crumpled him to his knees. His club fell from suddenly nerveless hands and he started to slip to the side. A gut-wrenching howl rang out as Mkai pulled the two daggers from the demon's back. He wiped the ichor on Gaptoz as the giant fell, convulsing in pain, his cries bouncing off the alley walls.

He took one last look at the fallen demon and turned back to the others. Mkai stopped short when he saw the two blocking the alley mouth. Rahale still shook his head but the sword was held firm in his grasp. Ortag wasn't moaning any longer, but from the tight snarl on his face and hand pressed to his side, the torment of the Ar'kt blade still ran through him. But his blade too, was held firm. From the resolve on their faces, Mkai didn't think he could provoke them to anger a second time.

"It's over now, Mkai," Ortag whispered, pain adding an edge to his voice.

"I've taken one of you; I'm good for at least one more," Mkai said, Gaptoz's howls fading into the silence of death. "Come, which of you is in a hurry to die next?"

"He is mine." Rahale bowed as Ortag stalked by. "Finally, I will taste your blood."

Mkai smiled tightly. "Really? That would be a first. There is something you should know about wounds made by the Ar'kt."

Ortag stopped as Mkai held up the blade.

"All have heard the first property. Any wound made by this blade will burn with never-ending pain." Mkai twisted the blade to catch an errant sunbeam so it gleamed in the gloom of the alley. "But few know of its second property, one even more devious."

Ortag stepped back as Mkai raised his other dagger. "It forges a connection with those whose blood it has tasted, a connection which can be used if you have the knowledge."

Sudden fear lit Ortag's eyes and he turned to flee. His turn faltered as Mkai ran the point of his dagger down the side of the Ar'kt. A shriek tore from Ortag's throat as he fell, pain buckling his knees. Both Ortag and Rahale stared as Mkai held up the Ar'kt blade.

"Properly used, the Ar'kt dagger shares its pain. What you do to the blade is shared by its victims." Mkai said grinding his dagger point into the blade. "And now it's just us," Mkai said as Ortag crumpled and started to writhe.

"Just as well. I owe you," Rahale said, sliding forward.

His confidence was warranted. Mkai knew Rahale was good with a blade. A sword against a dagger was usually a foregone conclusion. Mkai didn't have any tricks left. Skill alone would determine the outcome. But Mkai had something Rahale did not. Desperation.

He started to circle, daggers moving in and out, trying to draw a strike as Rahale turned in place, watching. Mkai eased his way closer and closer, aware of Rahale's feet and shoulders, watching for any hint of his intentions. He knew a strike would be signaled from there and he'd only have an instant to react.

"I thought about taking you alive," Rahale said, startling Mkai. "The reward would be greater if I did."

Mkai risked a darting glance at Rahale's eyes and was met with calm indifference.

"Ortag jumped at the chance to hunt you when I spread the word of your betrayal and, honestly, I expected a better showing from him. For all the years you've fought one another, I really thought he'd save me the trouble." Rahale spared a glance for the fallen Ortag, still racked with spasms, lost in the pain. "But no matter, I can and will take your life."

Mkai kept circling, trying to think of a plan. Something had been nagging in the back of his mind and he couldn't focus.

"Come, Mkai. I would have made it quick and painless but the longer you wait, the angrier I get. Soon it won't be an option for you."

With sudden insight, Mkai realized what his instincts were telling him. With a sword against a dagger, there was no reason for Rahale to delay, let alone try to distract Mkai. So why was he talking? He glanced once more and saw the still calm expression for what it was: fear, very tightly held. He feinted with the Ar'kt and the minute flinch confirmed his suspicions. Rahale was scared. It changed things.

"Then do it!" Mkai cried and leaped to the attack.

The startled look on Rahale's face as he quickly parried and backed away reassured Mkai and he kept up the attack. He thrust and slashed with his daggers, Rahale parrying desperately, flinching more and more at each slash of the Ar'kt dagger. Mkai drew the daggers in a complicated figure-eight and slashed with the blade of the Ar'kt. The snarling howl of agony bursting from Ortag startled Rahale. He quickly glanced at his fallen comrade. Mkai took advantage of the opening. Leaping forward, he thrust his dagger into Rahale's belly. Rahale grunted and his sword fell with a clang.

"This won't be quick," Mkai whispered and buried the Ar'kt dagger beside the other.

Rahale grabbed Mkai's hands and, raising his head, screamed in agony. Mkai twisted the blades and wrenched them free. Rahale dropped, gasping, his life's blood streaming from him.

That's two. Mkai turned and walked toward the fallen Ortag, still writhing on the ground.

"You were right, Ortag. It is over," Mkai said, kneeling.

Ortag looked up through eyes glazed with pain. Mkai waited until he saw the glimmer of sudden understanding in Ortag's eyes and plunged the Ar'kt dagger into his heart. A final shriek and spasm and it was done.

A gurgle and rattle at his side alerted Mkai that Rahale had joined the other two in death. Mkai stood, wiping the daggers clean and re-sheathing them. He looked at the bodies at his feet, glancing over at Gaptoz as the demon's corpse started to fade, the plane of Hell drawing the body back. He had a sudden thought and quickly searched the bodies. On Rahale, he found what he sought.

Got it! As'hame will need this. He held up the ring he'd pulled off Rahale's hand. He stood up and brushed off his knees. He watched as, slowly, the bodies of Ortag and Rahale started to fade as well. *At least that takes care of any evidence.* He shook his head, still in shocked disbelief. He couldn't believe he'd survived. He hadn't expected to. Sudden fear hit him.

Marie.

CHAPTER NINE

The familiar gloom of the bar comforted Rie. Her morning started with saving Paul and then sitting and talking with him for a couple hours. After coffee they walked around for a while before ending up sitting in the park, enjoying the sun. They finally separated after an early lunch, trading phone numbers and a rough plan to get together later in the week.

But it hadn't ended there for Rie. She'd found herself thinking about Paul as she walked the rest of the way home. Even after her normal restless sleep, thoughts of his blue eyes kept popping into her head. The way one corner of his mouth crooked up a little higher than the other when he smiled was disconcerting. She'd been attracted to men before but always on a casual basis. This had the feeling of something much more. She wasn't sure she liked it. After a day like this, she was happy to start her shift at Naco's, welcoming the distraction.

"Rie, a guy called for you."

"Thanks Tony. Did he leave a message?"

"Nope, just asked for you and then hung up."

"I get all the weirdos. Are you heading out?" she asked, stashing her small purse under the counter behind some bottles.

"Yeah, if that's okay. The wife said she has a surprise for me," he said with a grin.

"No problem, it's dead in here anyway. Get home and have fun." Rie said.

She shook her head as Tony bolted from the bar, a casual wave thrown over his shoulder. At six-foot four the image of him hurrying across the bar was comical. She scanned the place. Six pm and only two people sat in a corner booth. It seemed like it might shape up to be a slow night, not what she was hoping for. Tony left the back of the bar cleaned and organized, something she could always count on him for. The only drawback was it left very little for her to do.

She left home in a hurry and forgot her book. *Damn!* A quick check on the row of bottles and the cooler showed everything fully stocked. With a final glance around, she dragged a barstool behind the bar and perched on it, leaning back against the wall under the clock. She rested her head against the wall and let her mind wander over the day.

Paul's blue eyes filled her mind, and she remembered the aborted move he'd made when they'd parted ways.

Was he going to hug me? She wondered, surprised by a little thrill at the thought.

She found herself smiling. She hoped they met up again soon. Rie had left her cell number with him, something she very rarely did. Only a handful of people knew she even had a cell, and even fewer had her number. She hadn't even waited to see if he would ask for it and offered it up. But somehow, she knew they had been fated to meet and there was something about him, a connection she didn't understand. Rie didn't want him to disappear until she figured it out.

The bar lit up as someone opened the door and paused in the doorway. She couldn't make out anything from the silhouette and didn't recognize who it was until he stepped in, letting the door close behind him as he crossed toward her.

She slid off the stool with a half grin, reaching for an empty glass. "Kai!"

"Hello, Rie." His familiar voice made Rie flash back to the first time they met, in much the same circumstances.

*   *   *

Rie stepped in to the dark and gloomy bar, the smell of cigarette smoke and stale beer an assault on her nostrils. She grimaced to herself and made her way to the bar, the scowl on the hulking bartender giving her an idea of what was coming.

"You're late."

"Sorry, it was unavoidable, Steve," she said.

"It's been happening a lot lately."

"Like I said, it was unavoidable." This time she put some steel in her voice.

"Watch the attitude, little miss."

She glanced up at him when he stepped into her personal space.

"You should know better than to try to intimidate me, Steve. I said I was sorry, so don't push it."

Rie met his gaze calmly, letting the cold anger, which seemed to always be a part of her, shine in her eyes. She watched him stare at her with a sneer on his face that slowly disappeared. She saw him remember the rumors and the things said about her, the stories detailing what happened to those who pushed her. He finally stepped away, shoulders slumping in defeat. He simply nodded to her and walked away.

"He made a good choice there."

The voice, coming from behind her as it did, startled her but she showed nothing, turning to address the man behind her.

"He did, but how would you know that?"

"I asked around."

He said it simply, a shrug lifting one corner of the black, longshoreman jacket he wore, its thick collar framing his face. He stood a couple inches short of six feet, short dark hair accenting his cheekbones. Even in the gloom, she saw his green eyes. There was an unexpected openness in them. She leaned against the bar, her hand inches from her purse. Open eyes or not, she wasn't about to trust just anyone, especially if they'd been asking questions.

"Why would you be asking about me?" she asked quietly, poised to grab the 9mm from her purse if he had the wrong answer.

"I know Tommy, and he said you'd be able to help me."

"Help you how?"

"I am in need of some information and Tommy said you're the best in town."

She studied him for a moment, then straightened up, and held out her hand.

"No guarantees, but after I verify with Tommy, we'll see what I can do. My name is Rie."

"You can call me Kai."

*   *   *

She shook the memory loose with a smile. That was the beginning of a tentative relationship which slowly developed into friendship. Kai was one of the few people she considered a friend. He knew things about her and her past no one else did. The jacket was worn, but other than that very little had changed. There was a sadness in his eyes that was new but he still had the easy grin she had come to expect, and just seeing him made her lightened her day.

"It has been so long. I haven't heard anything from you for over three years. I'm glad you're back. I've missed you."

"It's good to be back in LA. I've missed this city," he said, easing himself onto a stool.

The careful way he moved, and the sadness she felt around him made her uneasy. In all the time she had known him, Kai always seemed carefree and cheerful; the fluid way he moved, almost dancing, seemed to emphasize his joy at life. Something had obviously changed; there was definitely something preying on his mind. *Which is probably why he's here.*

"Here you go, your usual. It's the same bottle from your last visit. No one else is crazy enough to drink this stuff," she said, sliding a glass of Malört in front of him, leaning against the bar, hiding her curiosity and worry as well as she could.

She watched as he sipped slowly, marveling at his ability to tolerate the strong schnapps. Rie caught the look of bleak loss flickering across Mkai's face as it always did at the first sip. Once again, she wondered what event in his past could bring such tortured memories every time he tasted it and why he kept drinking it. But, as she had every other time, she filed it away. He would tell her when he wanted to or he wouldn't; she wouldn't pry.

"Rie, I need your help."

The suddenness of his statement startled her, though she didn't allow it to show. Their meetings had a flow to them, a comfortable familiarity which eventually led to what he needed. The abruptness was jarring and she felt a sense of foreboding start to grow. *This has to be something important.*

"Of course, Kai. Have I ever let you down?" she smiled at him, hiding her misgivings.

"No, you never have," he said. "Can we talk someplace more discreet, away from prying eyes?"

She glanced at the pair in the booth, absorbed in their conversation, then back at Kai with a nod of her head toward them. "You're worried about those two? That's not like you. It must be something big." She waited for his nod before she continued. "Will the back stockroom do?"

"Yes, we don't need long."

Rie nodded, cast another glance at the pair down the bar, and, with her instincts fairly screaming, led Kai to the storeroom. She entered and turned to face him, raising a single eyebrow at the bar stool he carried into the room. He just smiled and slowly eased the door shut, leaving it just barely ajar.

"You're not going to close it all the way? I thought you wanted to this to be secret?"

"The need to hear if anyone approaches outweighs the security of a closed door," he said, setting the stool down in front of her, waving her to sit.

The unfamiliar formality and hinted danger made her suddenly glad to be sitting.

"We have known each for many long years, you and I," Kai continued, his tone still formal, "and in all that time, you never really asked about me, about why I needed what I did from you. You just gathered the information I asked for without question. I've always been grateful for that acceptance and silence but it's now time for you to know everything."

He paused, the continued drone of conversation from the two at the bar barely audible.

"We have always had a connection, I've felt, that makes you one of my favorites and one of only two I consider friends. That's why I can't ask you for what I need without letting you know exactly what you could be getting involved with."

Rie couldn't help the nerves making her legs fidget. But Kai was one of her oldest friends. "I used to wonder, back in the beginning, why you asked for what you did, each time you left with the information I found for you. For a long time I tried to piece together everything, trying to discover a pattern. But nothing ever made sense. There never seemed to be any connections. I did discover one thing, though."

She paused and captured his gaze with her own, the initial twisting of fear fading in favor of her trust in him. "The information I gathered for you, nothing bad ever came of it. In the odd case, the people involved were helped later on. Always in secret. No one was ever able to figure out who helped them, or why."

Rie sat up tall on the stool, her back firm with resolve, "It was then I accepted I would only find out if, and when, you decided to tell me. And it's also when I realized I trusted you, Kai. Everything that's happened since then, the things you've done for me, everything, it all reinforces that trust. You don't need to tell me anything more than you want to, but I'll be honest. I will be happy if you trust me enough in return to tell me everything."

She felt surprised, and more than a little concerned her words seemed to have the opposite effect than she expected. Instead of being reassured, Kai seemed saddened.

Tendrils of fear started creeping along her back when he said, "I hope you won't regret that. Hold that trust hard against what I am about to tell you. I am breaking a law older than you can imagine."

He paused, the haunted expression in his eyes making her heart ache. "I am not who or what you think I am. I am far older than I appear, far, far older. In all these long years, I have done the same thing as you: gathered information, varied and unrelated information, from around the world. You have been one of my contacts, and as I said, one of only two I considered something other than a tool."

Rie smiled. "I've always considered you a friend, Kai."

Kai nodded and continued. "You were what, eighteen when we met? You have changed, grown up in the years we've known each other. You never seemed to question the fact I have not changed in the same number of years."

"My view of you was colored, at first by my age, then with our familiarity. I have wondered but never gave it much thought. It's been my experience some people hide aging rather well," she said, wondering what point Kai was trying to make.

"That is true, but it is not what has made me appear the same after all this time. My name is Mkai and I am not . . . human." He said the words quietly.

CHAPTER TEN

Mkai watched Rie's eyes widen in surprise, and he reached to steady her as she swayed a bit on the stool. He pulled his arm back quickly, with a pang of sadness, when she shied away from his touch.

"I am thousands of years old. I walked the earth long before your oldest civilization, before the first of mankind crawled from the safety of the trees to walk and gather and hunt on the plains of the world. I watched your first steps and, with my brethren, every step since, marveling at the depth and growth possible."

"What are you?" she breathed.

"Ah, not as easy to answer today as it would have been as little as a week ago," Mkai said, "and one you may have a hard time accepting due to your religious views."

"Lack of, you mean. I've long been an atheist. It was one of the first things you knew about me, I think," she said. "What does that have to do with anything?"

The confusion he saw on her face made Mkai sigh.

"Yes, I have always understood your lack of faith, with the pain and grief of your past. It is not a surprise, even to me, that your faith would suffer for it. So I do understand how difficult this will be for you to accept."

"Religion has brought me nothing but pain and I have seen nothing to make me think it's anything but a skewed way to control people," Rie interrupted, anger and pain laced through her tone.

"I know, oh, I know so much better than you, my friend," Mkai said gently. "I know the depths of depravity to which people can sink. The horrors they inflict upon others, all in the name of religion."

"We've known each other a long time, Kai, and I know you well enough to know you wouldn't bring this up without reason," the hurt and anger in her eyes made Mkai wish he had another choice, "So spit it out, because I'm going to need a drink."

Mkai's heart twisted in his chest. So much pain and grief had been inflicted on this woman in the name of a twisted, offshoot religion. *Her mother has so much to answer for.*

"I, of all people, understand how you feel, and I wouldn't bring it up without cause. Please, for all the years you have known me, try to have an open mind to what I'm about to tell you." Mkai drew a deep breath.

"If it were anyone but you . . ."

"I know . . ."

"I don't know if you truly do. Religion has meant nothing but grief and pain to me. I was raised to believe in God, all while living through a hell few can understand. How could God, a kind and loving God, let those things happen to a child?" Mkai stepped back as Rie slid off her stool and started to pace. "How could He let those, those monsters do such sick and twisted things to me! I was an innocent and they tore that from me. They tore away my innocence even as they tore my virginity. And my ability to be a mother. All of it done in the name of their God. It is no simple thing, my rejection of God, and it goes far deeper than you can understand."

The anger and bone-deep sorrow in her voice echoed around the small room as Mkai stepped over to her and grasped her hands, dropping to one knee and stopping her pacing. He gazed up at her, letting all the compassion he had pour through his hands, willing her to see, to hear him.

"Oh, Rie, I know the hell that you've been through. I know the terrors visited upon you by the twisted and perverted minds of those you should have been able to trust. But, my dear, dear friend, that was not done in the name of God. Their actions were for their own sick and twisted needs. They simply used God as an excuse, as so many others have done. I can't claim to understand God, or why He allows such things, but I do know He exists. And I also know there is punishment for the monsters who commit crimes against innocence."

Mkai tightened his hold on her hands. "Child, there is a Heaven, and there is a Hell. Those who are good and kind do indeed go to Heaven. Those who are evil, those who commit murder, who rape, who steal, they are indeed banished to Hell." He kept his eyes locked with hers, hoping his next words would offer some kind of comfort, if not healing.

"Trust me when I say there is punishment for deeds like those. The men and women who forced such perversion on you are suffering for their actions," he said gently.

"How do you know? How can you guarantee that?" she asked so quietly he almost didn't hear.

"Because I saw to it."

"What?"

He led her back to the stool and settled her on it before continuing. "When you first told me what your childhood was like, I was angry. So very angry. I went to your hometown. Went to find out what I could."

Mkai stopped for a moment to step to the door and glance out at the bar. Other than the two engrossed in conversation in their booth, the bar remained empty. He turned back to where Rie sat on the stool, hands clasped tightly against the pain, eyes filled with tears yet unfallen.

"I was, because of what I am, able to find out a great deal. They didn't stop after you fled. They continued with their rape and torture, claiming they were cleansing the evil. But they went too far. They killed a couple of young girls." Mkai grimaced, feeling his stomach twist. "Murder is a sin, not to mention the rest. It didn't take much effort to pass along the right information to the authorities. When the FBI arrived to arrest the group, they resisted and they all died in the ensuing gunfire. They are all currently in Hell, suffering a just punishment for their actions in life. I have seen this with my own eyes."

Tears began to slip down Rie's cheeks as Mkai placed his hands on her shoulders. "I know it is little comfort, Rie, but I made sure they were punished for what they did to you. There is justice."

She covered her face with her hands and he gathered her to his chest as she wept, wept for innocence long lost but finally avenged. He let her cry herself out while thinking about how to tell her the rest.

She finally sat back, scrubbing the tears from her eyes. "I thank you. If what you say is true, it means more than you'll ever know. But there is more to it, isn't there? You didn't just come to tell me something that happened years ago. You said 'because of what you are' and that you saw them with your own eyes. What did you mean?"

Mkai felt a little apprehensive as he stared into her tear-reddened eyes. But he needed her, so what choice did he have? "As I said, there is a Heaven, and a Hell, as well as all the conditions which go with them. Angels and demons. In this, at least, the Bible is partly correct."

Rie sat back on the stool and just watched him. Mkai didn't know quite how to interpret her expression. "There was a war in Heaven, a terrible one, sweeping all of Heaven into the conflict. Few escaped unscathed. I, and others like me, were not so fortunate. Satan, as most humans name him, or more properly, Samael, did rebel against God, and in losing, was cast out. Those who sided with him, fell with him."

He paused, fear tracing down his spine. *You've gone this far and it's too late to change your mind.* Mkai met Rie's eyes, eyes clouded with questions, pain, and, perhaps, a little fear.

"I was one of them. I never rebelled directly against God, but I did gather information for those I should not have, information that resulted in the destruction of my brothers and sisters. Because of this, I did accept my punishment. I was banished from Heaven and given to an eternity of Hell, with the earthly plane the only solace from the darkness. I have spent all these years gathering information to try to make amends for the choices I made. Sometimes using it to right the wrongs of the world."

"A demon?" she asked, more than a little fear in her eyes.

He quietly looked at her for a moment, "Yes, I am a demon now. But I was an angel once. I am still the Kai you've known all these years. I am not evil."

He waited for her to nod before continuing, "It was this search for information which led me to uncover what few know. The world is in peril. The War is in danger of beginning again but this time it will be fought with the damned Souls of Man. It threatens all of creation and I need your help to stop it."

Rie's eyes widened as Mkai went on. "There is a new demon on the throne of Hell and her new orders are to corrupt and damn as many souls as possible. Once those souls are in Hell they are converted into an army, an army which will invade Heaven. She believes God will be defenseless against her."

He stopped for a moment, gathering his thoughts, pacing up and down the small room while Rie stayed quiet. Mkai wasn't sure if this was a bad thing or a good thing.

"That, in itself, is bad enough, but it is far more critical. God's Son has been sent to earth again, sent to save you once more. He is unaware of His lineage. And that is the second goal of Hell—orders to find Him and corrupt Him. Then, as a damned soul, He will lead the forces of Hell into Heaven against His Father."

"Jesus has been sent to die on the cross again? What will that serve?" she interrupted.

Mkai stopped his pacing at her question. "I don't know God's plan for Him, just that He's been sent. This is where you come in, Rie. I need your help, your contacts, and the information you can gather to help me find Him. I am not alone in this. There is an order of angels who refused to partake in the War and turned their back to Heaven, coming to Earth to protect mankind." He could see the disbelief on Rie's face, but went on. "I met with one of them, As'hame by name, and he is sweeping the city to see if he can locate God's Son, for protection. My information says the Son was sent to L.A. It is here that the Son of God is supposed to reveal Himself. This has not yet happened and we *must* find Him."

"Kai, I would dearly love to believe you. I would." Rie's face still bore the tracks of tears visible on her cheeks. "But this is expecting a lot. I don't know if I can believe all of it, especially about the Son of God and all that."

"I know. I wish there was a way to prove it." Mkai felt like wringing his hands but kept still. Either the years of trust would hold, or they would not.

"It's not really necessary, not right now."

"What do you mean?" He felt a spark of hope.

Rie smiled at him, "I never knew why you needed the information I've gathered for you before and that hasn't changed. I can help you without believing in your reasons."

"It will be dangerous, Rie, that's why I had to tell you," Mkai said, concern drawing his brows together. "I'm not the only one searching for him. And the others wouldn't hesitate to kill or torture you if they suspected you knew anything."

"I've dealt with dangerous people before."

"But these will not be people," he said. "They are demons. At least believe that much. If you are willing to help you must be more careful than you've ever been. They can't even get the faintest whiff you may be involved."

He wavered and then continued. "They have killed other contacts of mine, tortured and killed them trying to get information."

Rie nodded. "I understand. I will be as careful as I can. So how can I help? Do you have a name or description?" she asked, leaning forward, resting an elbow on her raised leg. "Obviously the more information you can give me, the easier it will be to find Him."

Mkai breathed a sigh of relief. He should have known. Rie was a fighter, always had been. "Unfortunately, we know next to nothing. I know He will be in His mid to late twenties, and is in L.A.. That is everything we know about Him. But it is not how we will find Him. It will be His actions, His behavior, which will reveal Him. He is the Son of God and His influence will show. I need you to look for the unexplained, the weird, and unnatural. I cannot stress enough how important it is. We must find Him first. His powers may keep Him hidden to a certain point, and will probably act to keep Him safe. But if He is found before He fully understands who He is, He can be taken and that would be a catastrophe for the world."

"I'll do the best I can," Rie said, standing, "Have a little faith." She winked.

Mkai smiled slightly at her little joke. *She is still able to make jokes, but this is no joking matter. Still, perhaps she will find peace through this, after all.*

CHAPTER ELEVEN

As'hame landed on the rooftop, his frustration echoed in the audible thump of his boots. Two days, two days he'd been searching. He'd covered virtually every foot of the sprawling city he protected and didn't sense even a hint of his quarry. With his attention focused, he should have been able to pinpoint at least the rough area, but nothing. He sensed some demonic energy around downtown earlier in the day, but his search was too important so he didn't stop to investigate. After finally giving up for the moment, he turned his attention to tracking Mkai. It turned out to be easy, even without the aura of his bracelet. *I hope Mkai had better luck with his mission.*

He found him walking down Beacon Avenue, palm trees lining the side of the street, appearing like he was just another human. Mkai was obviously lost in thought as As'hame stepped out between buildings.

"Mkai."

"As'hame! I was wondering when you'd be back. Did you have any luck?" Mkai seemed relieved, making As'hame curious about how his tasks had gone.

As'hame shook his head. "Nothing, not even a glimmer. We are not going to be able to find him by simply walking the streets. How did it go for you?"

"I started to contact my people and ran into trouble." Mkai said grimly. "After you left, a . . . colleague, Rahale, accosted me. He had been following me and wanted to know what I was doing."

Mkai's speech became more formal as he outlined the last couple day's events. "It appears that, of the net I had active here, only two remain alive. A demon called Drekor, particularly vicious and cruel, even by the standards of Hell, has slaughtered the rest."

"Only two? How did those two remain safe?" As'hame asked.

"Because I cared for them, they meant . . . mean something more to me. I took special care to keep our relationship secret." Mkai seemed a bit abashed to admit this to As'hame.

The angel merely nodded. "Understandable. These humans find a way to become important to us. It is part of the reason why my brethren and I are here. Go on, how did you discover this?"

"First, I found the remains of one contact and on the way to another one, Rahale caught up with me again. And he brought friends."

"So that was the disturbance I felt," As'hame said placing his hand on Mkai's shoulder. "I am sorry. If I had realized you were in danger, I would have come."

"It's all right. I can handle myself. Besides, your quest was more important. As it turned out, I had no need of help." Mkai seemed to stand taller. As'hame repressed an amused grin.

"You defeated all three? Quite impressive. Even I might hesitate to face three at once. Who were they?"

"Ortag and his dim-witted lackey, Gaptoz," Mkai said with a grimace.

In spite of himself, As'hame actually was impressed. "I have heard the names, usually attached to atrocities turning my stomach. You defeated . . ."

"Killed. With the Ar'kt dagger."

"The Ar'kt dagger? You have some surprises, I see." As'hame couldn't help wondering what other surprises this demon might have in store. "It is an exceptional weapon, and the pain? Is that true or is it simply myth?"

"Oh, the pain it causes is real, all three could attest to that. It is the main reason I was able to vanquish them."

"Well done. If you had not already had it, your actions would earn my gratitude. Those three deserved death a long time ago." As'hame said. "Did you get to your other contact?"

"Yes, eventually. I had to wait for her to return to her work. She agreed to help in the search. She does not fully believe, but as she put it, her belief has no bearing on her ability to help."

"At this point, she is correct. Her belief is not necessary. And your other remaining contact, how are they aiding our search?"

"Roger deals with things, not information." Mkai said, "I gave him a list of requirements and he will provide everything. He has never let me down."

"Excellent. Thank you. You have done very well with your people. I think it is time to involve my own. You seem to have everything under control for now, and we have time while your contacts work. It should not take me more than a day to reach the Council and hopefully not longer than that to convince them." As'hame paused a moment to think. "I will return in four to five days. Regardless of whether the Council agrees, I will return in no more than six days. I hope to return sooner, and with reinforcements. This fight is far too important, and will get far too large for just the two of us. Watch for me." He nodded to Mkai and turned to leave.

"Wait!" the urgency in Mkai's voice stopped As'hame, and he looked quizzically at his ally. "There's one more thing you should know. Rahale followed me to our first meeting and was close enough to know you for what you are."

"And I did not sense him? How?" As'hame asked, startled. If the demons were able to hide their presence from him, the search would become much more dangerous.

"I managed to get the answer out of him before he escaped," Mkai said. "A ring. After I killed him and the others I found it while searching his body."

"A simple ring?"

"Yes. I don't fully understand how it works, but try to sense me." Mkai pulled the ring he had taken off Rahale's body from his pocket.

As'hame opened his senses carefully until he felt the demonic energy emitting from Mkai despite the human glamour, and then nodded. He could barely control his shock as Mkai disappeared from his senses when he slipped the ring on his finger.

"If it were not for my eyes, I would not believe you stand before me," As'hame said. "Indeed, this is not good news, but I am grateful you found out when you did. It could have turned disastrous for us if we were not aware."

"I agree. I don't know how many rings exist, or if they have other methods of hiding themselves, but I thought you should know." Mkai removed the ring and once again As'hame felt his presence.

"Keep the ring; it may come in handy later. Are there any more revelations you have to share?" As'hame asked. Mkai shook his head. "Then I thank you, and I will be back soon. Watch your back."

The two exchanged a final handshake, and, with a powerful leap, As'hame sprang to the sky. His unfurled wings caught the air and three beats later he was high in the sky, his beloved city below.

As he sped through the air, As'hame focused on the information he'd just learned from Mkai and how to present it to the Council. How to convince them of the coming struggle and how to best react? All of this was based on the word of a demon and, while As'hame trusted his instincts, he wasn't sure the Council would. They had been out of touch with the world for hundreds of years as they focused on managing the As'rai. As'hame feared such an attitude would affect their judgment in regard to the severity of this problem.

His wings flapped tirelessly as he gathered his thoughts and began to form his speech. He had close to a solid day of flying ahead of him to come up with the words needed to sway the Council to support him. He only hoped it would be enough.

At last, the lights of New York appeared on the horizon. As'hame still marveled at the Council's location, the distinctive crown of the Chrysler building recognizable in the distance. Taking the top, uninhabited floors in such a familiar landmark made it an ideal meeting location for the As'rai and it always signified, at least to him, the connection they had with the humans they watched and guarded. He landed softly on the seventy-third floor, the As'rai on duty already opening the window.

"Welcome, As'hame. It has been too long since you have been here," a familiar voice greeted him as he stepped in.

"Ti'raon!" As'hame said, smiling as he stepped forward to hug one of his oldest friends.

He held her at arm's length. Her short, brown hair fell loosely, not quite to her shoulders, and her green eyes held a warmth he had missed.

"You appear well, my friend. It has been far too long."

"It has," she said.

"Nice boots," he said with a grin looking pointedly at the high-heeled footwear, adding at least four inches to her height.

She just rolled her eyes at him.

"How is Houston?" As'hame asked.

"Hot. And humid."

"You have been to hotter places," he chuckled.

"Yes, Jerusalem was much hotter, but drier."

"What are you doing here? Last I heard, you had shown a rather large group of demons Houston was ours. What brings you to the Council?"

"Just reporting in. There seems to be an increase in activity and, from what I hear, it is not only Houston," she said grimly. "Something is going on and the Council is trying to determine what."

"I have information which may shed some light. Do you have to leave right away or are you able to stay? You, of all of us, should hear what I have to say," As'hame said as they stepped into the Council's anteroom.

"I was on my way back to Houston when you entered, but I can wait."

He ignored the unasked question in her eyes and greeted a familiar friend. "T'alw, it has been a while."

"As'hame! Welcome, the Council did not realize you were coming." T'alw stood from his desk. "Ti'raon, did you not already report?"

She nodded and gestured to As'hame.

"Indeed, I was not summoned but I have much to share and I believe Ti'raon should hear it as well," As'hame said before she could answer.

"Of course, As'hame, the Council is free at the moment. But we would welcome you regardless." T'alw swung open the heavy door.

As'hame nodded his gratitude as he stepped into the chamber.

He felt Ti'raon stop behind him as he walked to the center of the chamber, the closing of the door audible in the silence. The thud of his boots on the hardwood floor echoed softly as he walked. He felt awed, as always, by this room. Of all the places the As'rai had called home, this one, in the middle of one the most influential cities of the world, spoke to him the most.

Instead of simply overlaying what man had wrought with materials, fabrics, or patterns comfortable and familiar to the As'rai dwelling here, effort was made to incorporate what Man had created into the final design and use of the room. Here, as in no other place in the world, the strong, sometimes harsh lines of Man merged, and were complemented by the smooth, curved elegance representative of the As'rai.

The combination had, at first, been too at odds, but through time As'hame had come to recognize the beauty and the symbolism presented so simply. Here was the epitome of their order. To work with Man, to be part of their world, not separated like all other Angelic orders.

He halted in the middle of the room, his booted feet resting on the inlaid silver symbol of his order where it had been painstakingly installed into the wood planks of the floor. He always loved the purity of silver and here it shone brighter than anywhere else as if to say that here, here was the heart of everything the As'rai stood for.

As'hame gazed around the chamber, breathing in the calm he always felt when surrounded by the marks of his order's dedication to the safety of Man. His own certainty of their mission was renewed each time. He inhaled deeply and, exhaling, bowed slowly to the Council in front of him.

CHAPTER TWELVE

"Welcome, As'hame. It has been long since you have visited us. Now, as always, you are welcome."

The ritual greeting was offered by the head of the Council with a bow. One by one, the other three members bowed in turn.

"Thank you, Ea'mol, for the gracious greeting." As'hame bowed in response. "I only hope, after I share my news, you will feel the same."

The Council exchanged glances, then Ea'mol spoke again. "This Council has always trusted your word, As'hame. We will listen to what you have to say without judgment. Be not afraid to speak your mind to us."

As'hame sighed with relief. With formalities completed, he could get to his point. "Thank you. My news is indeed dire, but I am eased by your graciousness. As Ti'raon has just informed me, you have called in As'rai from around the country," As'hame began.

"Not just this country," said a voice from behind him.

As'hame turned to see a familiar figure standing beside Ti'raon. Ro'molr. He bulked large beside Ti'raon, making her seem even slighter than she was, his familiar grin firmly set.

"Yes, Ro'molr, you are correct. We have called in As'rai from around the world, As'hame, but please continue," Ea'mol said with exasperation.

Not all As'rai appreciated Ro'molr and his sense of humor. But it was one of the traits As'hame appreciated the most. He himself had a tendency to be too serious at times, but Ro'molr was adept at inducing As'hame to relax and see the lighter side of things.

As'hame turned back to the council. "You have called in the As'rai because of reports of increased demon activity. I do not yet know what the others have reported, but we have seen the same increase in Los Angeles. What is more, I know the reason why."

His words fell into the silence and he felt every eye on him, watching, waiting.

"I was contacted a demon by the name of Mkai," As'hame continued.

"A demon! And you bothered to talk to him before you killed him?" Ho'fal cried, jumping to his feet.

As'hame saw the rage on the council member's face. He remembered Ho'fal standing in this very chamber, tears of grief and pain pouring down his cheeks as he recounted the destruction wrought upon the city of Hamoukar. Demons were responsible, and Ho'fal had never forgotten, had never forgiven. His hatred for them for the destruction of the city he protected burned fiercely, even after more than five thousand years.

"I did not kill him. I have come across him several times over these long years of guarding Man, and he has always left at my command and has never, to my knowledge caused any chaos or death, to us or to Man," As'hame stated.

"I find that hard to believe. He is a demon and you should have destroyed him." Ho'fal said glaring across the chamber, anger thick in his voice.

"I, too, have had dealings with this Mkai. I agree, he has never caused us trouble," Ro'molr said into the silence.

"He gathers information as far as I have been able to figure out," Ti'raon added, "I have followed him to determine his actions, and that is all he has ever done. Gather information. He never seemed to share it with anyone and I have seen him shun and avoid other demons. I do believe he is different."

As'hame felt grateful for their unexpected support but knew he had to convince the Council. "He had some extremely dire news and, because of our past, hurried to share it with me at the risk of his own life. Indeed, he was attacked for doing so." Ho'fal returned to his seat, scowling. "Hell has a new Master and a new goal."

As'hame's words fell like stones in a pool. He watched the ripples of thought as the Council before him heard and absorbed his words.

"Her name is Kalia and her new mandate, as was told to me, is to fill Hell with as many corrupted souls as possible, to damn as many people as possible. And once the damned are in Hell, they are being tortured and converted until they give over and join Hell gladly. An army is being built, rank and file, from the souls of Man. With one purpose." As'hame paused and looked at the councilors one at a time, ensuring he had their full attention, waiting for the question he knew they had to ask.

"Why does Hell need an army?" Ea'mol said quietly, leaning forward.

"For war. She is building an army of the souls of Man, to go against God. She plans on picking up where Samael failed, but this time with the souls of God's children."

"What?" Ea'mol bellowed, leaping to his feet, his aura shining forth, suddenly clad in armor. His cry was echoed from the Council as they too, jumped to their feet in shock.

"Wait!" As'hame cried, motioning for silence, "There is more!"

Slowly, the Council settled, murmuring quietly to each other. As'hame noted Ho'fal whispering in the ear of Di'sha and wondered what they were planning. Those two worked together often, always for the good of the As'rai, but they did enjoy surprising everyone else.

"What more could there be? This is already enough to jeopardize everything we know," Ea'mol said, remaining on his feet, his hand resting on the hilt of the sword at his waist.

"God has decided Mankind needs another chance and has sent His Son down once more."

The silence was overwhelming, barely disturbed as Ea'mol fell with a rattle of armor into his chair.

"The Savior of Man is once again on earth, unaware of who He is, and the demons from Hell are searching for Him," As'hame said, breaking the silence.

As'hame nodded at Ea'mol as sudden understanding filled his eyes with fear. "They are searching for Him. To steal and corrupt Him and once He is damned, to lead their army into Heaven."

The silence was almost painful, anguish filling the eyes of all present as they absorbed the news and worked through consequences.

"This is indeed grave news, As'hame. We thank you for hurrying to bring us this," Ea'mol finally said, "there is much to do, before we can even begin searching for Him."

"Wait, Ea'mol, there is one last thing," As'hame said holding up his hand. "Searching is required, but we do know at least a place to start. He has been sent to Los Angeles. He is in my city."

"We know this? Know it for sure?" Ea'mol asked.

"Yes. I have destroyed over twenty demons in just the last week. Mkai faced and killed three on his own. They are invading my city in their search. And I cannot protect it, or Him, alone."

"You will not be alone." As'hame heard the declaration from behind him and he turned to see both Ti'raon and Ro'molr nod, clothed in armor.

He nodded back gratefully before turning back to the Council. "We need to gather, all of us from across the world. Nothing can be as important as this. We must get to Los Angeles. We must find Him and keep Him safe."

"I do not think there is any disagreement," Ea'mol said. "In fact, there is no time to waste. Organization, we can handle. How soon can you return to your city to continue the search?"

"I have already crossed the city several times and I did not feel even the slightest glimmer of His presence, and I should have," As'hame said. "Somehow, He is shielded from me."

"You would not detect Him," Ti'raon said behind him, "He will have something, an amulet, a ring, or a brooch, something to ward him. It was a copper ring in Jerusalem."

As'hame remembered the torment Ti'raon went through when God sent His Son to earth to die for Man's sins. She had been forbidden to interfere and, instead, stood as witness, in anguish, as he was sacrificed for Mankind. Ro'molr reached out and gripped her shoulder and nodded as As'hame turned back to the Council.

"Perhaps with the three of you, as well as this Mkai, you will be able to find Him. We will organize and send other members of the As'rai to you as quickly as we can," Ea'mol said, stepping from around the table. "We can't pull everyone out; it will leave too many cities vulnerable. But the squads of La'sfo will be sent and as many others as can be spared."

"It will take time to organize but it will be done." Di'sha spoke up, standing, "Ho'fal and I have already been discussing the logistics and will organize it ourselves."

"Leaving myself and Ba'yar free to bring the As'rai to you when we have gathered," Ea'mol said coming up to As'hame.

"Thank you, thank you all." As'hame said, "If you can, send the La'sfo right away. I don't think we will have to time to wait for all to gather. We will need all the help we can get, and as soon as possible."

"You will have it. The La'sfo will be yours as quickly as we can contact them. We will send them directly to you. The As'rai scattered across North America we will also send on to you in small groups as they gather. We will gather those As'rai in Europe and Africa and hold them here. From Asia and Australia we will send them across the

Pacific to the west coast. Then you will have reinforcements coming from both directions." Ea'mol said.

"Excellent plan, one way or another I will have As'rai to help me keep him safe. Thank you," As'hame replied with a short bow.

"We will also look for a stronghold. We have never faced anything like this before so we may have to improvise, if it comes to that. Communication should not be too difficult. Few of us have embraced technology fully, but almost all have cell phones or have arranged message drops. We can spread the word much faster today than ever before. We will start as soon as we are done here," Ba'yar added.

Ea'mol clasped As'hame's arm. "Be safe and get us word if possible. We will join you soon."

"Thank you. I was not sure if I would be believed. This is all based on the word of a demon, after all," As'hame admitted.

"Why would you worry? Do you not know? You are the greatest of us," Ea'mol said squeezing As'hame's shoulder.

As'hame looked around in surprise as the other three council members joined Ea'mol. All nodded in agreement to Ea'mol's final word.

"It is only your focus on duty that has stopped us from calling you to a seat on our Council," Ba'yar said.

"You have long been the role model to which we all aspire, and the fact you never realized it is partly why," Di'sha said from where she stood beside Ho'fal. "We would follow you without question."

As'hame felt humbled by their words and bowed. "I am not worthy of such praise but I will try to not disappoint."

"We would, indeed, storm Hell's Gate itself at your command," Ti'raon quietly uttered.

"But don't let it go to your head," came Ro'molr's reply with a grin.

"Now, go. We will be there as soon as we can." Ea'mol ushered them from the chamber. "Good luck; be safe. Find Him."

As'hame turned as the door closed, leaving him with his two closest friends. "We're going to be in it this time. The last war we avoided by coming Earth. We have no such choice here. There can be no quarter, no mercy, if the worlds are to survive."

"We know, As'hame. We would be nowhere but by your side." As'hame felt his heart lift for the first time since his initial conversation with Mkai.

"Then we fly hard and as fast as we can," As'hame said as he stepped to the ledge.

"Last one there buys the beer!" Ro'molr cried leaping off the roof.

As'hame shared a wry glance with Ti'raon. Interaction with humans had definitely changed Ro'molr.

He leapt from the ledge, his wings unfurling. *We have a chance now*, his wings catching the air and thrusting him into the night sky. *We have a chance.*

CHAPTER THIRTEEN

"Hello?"

"Hi, Rie, it's Paul."

"Oh. Hi, Paul!"

Paul felt a flutter at the smile in her voice and the thrill of hearing Rie speak his name. "I'm just getting off work and wondered if you'd like to get coffee or breakfast?"

He hadn't wanted to call too soon but she was all he could think about. Paul marveled at how his mood changed since spending part of the day with her. He felt happy, happier than he had been in a long time. Even some of the people at work had commented on his change in attitude.

"Sure, I'm just leaving work myself. Where?"

"I know a great little breakfast place close to Camacho." Paul said, trying to keep the nervousness out of his voice.

"Sounds good, meet you in front and then you can lead the way?"

"Excellent. See you in twenty."

Paul disconnected with a grin and slipped his phone in his pocket as he strode down the street. His pace increased as he realized he was really looking forward to seeing Rie. It had been difficult to wait to call her, but he hadn't wanted to freak her out. Throw in his own fears of rushing too fast and waiting was definitely the smarter move. Still, he couldn't help but grin at the excitement and butterflies in his stomach at the thought of seeing her again.

The light stopped him at the corner and he stood for a moment, remembering the spot where they first met. He had, as any typical boy, his share of cuts, scrapes and bruises growing up but he had never felt like his life had ever really been in danger. That day was the closest he'd ever been to dying, or even being badly hurt. It still shook him a little when he thought of it. The tiniest thing could have changed the day; if he'd walked a little faster, if she had reached out too slowly to stop him.

Thinking it over the last couple days, he was slowly beginning to believe Rie's conviction they were fated to meet. He thought about why he hadn't gone home on the morning they met. He realized that the ache and loneliness he associated with his apartment wasn't there anymore. *If nothing else, Rie helped you get past that.* He laughed, *besides saving you, that is.*

The light flashed to "Walk" and, after looking carefully both ways, Paul hurried across the street, determined to enjoy the day. He made it to Camacho without trouble and he didn't even try to stop the genuine smile from spreading across his face at Rie's approach.

"No traffic incidents?" she asked, smiling.

"Nope. You showed me I can never be too careful. The diner is around the corner and up a block or so."

"Then let's go."

They set off and soon he was laughing as Rie started describing some of the characters she'd seen at her bar.

"So here he was, almost six and a half feet tall, about three hundred pounds and wearing a complete cowboy outfit. Boots, hat, AND chaps, and all of it either a dark chocolate brown or bright pink!"

The image in his head from her description made Paul chuckle, turning into outright laughter as she continued.

"Have you ever seen Neapolitan ice cream? It was totally like that! And he talked to everyone with this John Wayne drawl." Rie said, "He really was the nicest guy, very polite and all, but oh, the stares he got!"

"That must have been something," Paul said. "I may have to come and check out this bar of yours."

"I'd like that," she said, meeting his eyes before quickly looking away.

A flush threatened to creep across his cheeks and Paul floundered, trying to think of something witty to say. Normally, he never had a problem talking with women. *What's wrong with me? Why is this one so different?*

"It's just over there," he finally managed to get out, pointing up the street where a huge sign stood on the sidewalk.

She grinned and the flush burst out, heat rising in his cheeks. She shook her head and patted his arm, making him blush even more. The absurdity made him chuckle again and he shook his head as he opened the door for her.

She stepped into the cafe and stopped at the scowl greeting her. The woman by the till was obviously not having a good day. She sent Paul a look as he came in behind her. He just patted her arm as he stepped up to the woman.

"Good morning," he said with a smile.

Rie watched as the woman's scowl changed, her lips curving upwards, the storm in her eyes fading.

"Good morning to you. How can I help you?"

"I would like a table for two please, preferably a booth," he said waving Rie forward, "I wanted to show my friend the best breakfast in the city."

"Why thank you," she said with a big smile, "we really appreciate that. We do our best to keep our customers happy. I will have someone take you to your table."

Rie looked back and forth between Paul and the hostess, surprised and a little amazed at the drastic change in behavior. To go from obviously angry at the world to smiling and friendly in such a short time was not something she saw happen often. *There really is something special about Paul.*

A white haired waitress with the incongruous name tag "Candy" led them to a table by the window and they settled in after ordering coffee.

"What's good? I've never been here," Rie asked, opening her menu.

"Almost everything, but stay away from the El Rancho omelet unless you really like spicy," Paul said.

Rie glanced up with a quick grin before turning back to her menu.

"Have you decided, dears?" the waitress asked as she set their coffee on the table.

"I'd like the burger, with American cheddar and bacon, no tomato, extra pickles, and fries, please," Rie said.

"Would you like gravy?"

"Yes, please."

"And for you?" Candy asked, a twinkle in her eye when she turned to Paul.

He fought another blush; the knowing twinkle in her eyes told him Candy was happy to see him here with a woman, instead of alone. He quickly ordered his regular scrambled eggs, chunky potatoes, sausage, and brown toast with a side of bacon.

"Thank you. Your food won't take too long."

"Thank you," Paul said as Candy walked away, tucking the pen and pad into her apron.

"Candy, huh . . ." Rie whispered to Paul as their waitress walked away.

"Yeah, it's rather funny. They have a Candy, a Flo, an Alice, and a Carla. From what I can figure out, none of them are their actual real names. The owner has a thing for TV waitress names so he chooses a 'name' for each waitress he hires and that's the name tag they get."

"Really? That actually does sound rather funny," Rie said, sitting back and taking a sip of her coffee. "Do you come here often?"

"A couple times a month," Paul said, "Candy is one of the best here but they're all very good."

Rie smiled at him and picked up her coffee.

"So . . . burger?" he asked, watching her.

"Yeah, I like to see people's reactions when I order something like that when everyone else is ordering breakfast."

"Not me. I love breakfast food. Pancakes, waffles, eggs, bacon, sausage, toast, love them all." Paul said chuckling, "I'd have breakfast for dinner if I could."

Paul stifled a happy sigh as his nervousness slowly flowed away and he started to relax.

"I'm glad you called."

"I figured two days was past the stalker line so it was safe."

"Yes, two days is the safe number of days to wait," Rie said. "I've been really busy anyway so it worked out well."

"Busy? The bar has been crazy?" Paul asked, leaning forward.

"Yeah. It seems everyone in L.A. wanted to drink at the same time and they all picked Naco's. But not just that."

Paul raised an eyebrow as she paused and, taking a sip of coffee, waited for her to continue. He watched her look at him over her cup, obviously stalling for time. Paul was already beginning to recognize it as a characteristic habit as she shrugged.

"It's not just the bar keeping me busy," she started, "I also gather information. Where I work, the people I know, I can usually find out what's going on in the city. A guy I've known for years pays me very well for it."

He nodded for her to continue.

"I haven't heard from him in a while but he showed up a couple days ago. The day we met, actually. He needs my help so that's what I've been doing."

She fell silent as Candy approached, arms laden with plates. Her years of experience were obvious as she quickly set their meals down.

"Burger with bacon and cheese, hold the tomato with extra pickles." she said as she set Rie's plate down, "And of course, gravy for the fries."

"Thank you," Rie said, settling a napkin in her lap.

"And your regular order, scrambled eggs with sausage, toast, and bacon." The emphasis she put on 'and' made Paul smile like it always did. "I had them add a little cheese to your eggs and an extra piece or two of bacon may have landed on your plate somehow."

Paul grinned as Candy set his meal down, "Aw thank you, Candy. You always take such good care of me."

"Of course I do, dear," she said with a wink. "You two enjoy your breakfast; I'll be back in bit to check on you."

Paul grinned as she walked away and then glanced at Rie.

"A couple times a month?"

"Well, ok, maybe a little more often than that."

"It's nice being a regular, especially in place where they obviously take care of you."

"Yes, it is. I feel at home here. They're all really great people."

"It shows," she said, popping a fry in her mouth, "and the fries are fantastic."

"They are," he said, stabbing some chunky potatoes on his fork. "Everything is good here."

Paul chewed as he watched her pick up her burger and take a bite, her eyes on him as she chewed. He toyed with his fork before setting it down to grab his glass of water.

"That's kinda cool," Paul said, finally breaking the silence.

Rie looked at him, a question in her eyes.

He tried to explain. "Helping your friend. Working where I do, I have been . . . exposed, I guess, to some of what goes on in the city, but I've never really been involved directly. You actually fit in that world, I can see it. From the moment we met, I've known you're tough. You're not like most of the women I know: afraid of breaking a nail or getting dirty, so concerned with appearances they forget how to live."

He paused and then grinned.

"I really like that."

"Oh, I put on nail hardener so I don't have to worry about breaking them" she said with a smile drawing a chuckle from him.

"Is it dangerous, what you're doing?" Paul asked, trying to disguise the worry he felt at the thought.

"Not really. The areas I have to go aren't always the best but the people I talk to usually aren't dangerous."

"Is it inappropriate to ask what kind of information you're searching for?"

"I . . ." she paused, clearly gathering her thoughts, "I've never told anyone what I do. I'm not sure if I should tell you. I don't want to get you involved."

Paul nodded, "I understand. After all, we did just meet."

"Oh, it's not that I don't trust you," she interrupted. "For some reason, I do." She seemed surprised by her own words.

He couldn't help but smile at the shy way she avoided his eyes. He tore off a piece of toast and popped it in his mouth.

"I trust you, but I don't want to complicate your life. Knowledge can be dangerous in this town, distracting at the very least. Which, for you, is dangerous," Rie finished with a grin.

"Ha! Yeah, distractions and traffic and I don't really get along," Paul said.

"This time, it's not just information I'm looking for. It's actually a person I'm trying to find, or at least information about them."

"A person? As big as L.A. is, how could you ever find one single person?" he said, spearing the last piece of sausage.

"It's surprisingly easy at times," she said. "People always cause ripples around them as they go through their everyday lives. And other people notice these ripples. For example, you buy coffee and, say, you order something non-standard, or you stand out from the norm, either physically or by wearing something distinctive. The barista will remember you, even if vaguely. You buy something from a corner vendor, same thing."

He nodded in understanding.

"These are the people I talk to, or more accurately, I know people who talk to them." Rie picked up a French fry and nibbled. "In this way, I can actually reach out across the city and, sometimes in a very short time, find almost anyone."

"Wow, you make it seem so simple." Paul didn't try to hide the note of awe in his voice. "So this person you're looking for, how quickly will you find them?"

"Oh, this one isn't going to be that easy. Normally, I have a certain amount of information making it easier. This time, all I know is he's male, probably in his twenties," she said picking up the last bite of burger. "That's almost all I have to go on."

"A twenty-something man? In L.A.?" Paul asked. "That's impossible. Hell, look around us, there's easily eight guys matching that description. Even I do!"

"I know. The only other thing I was told," she paused, "my friend told me weird things might happen around this guy."

"Weird things?" Paul felt a strange sensation in his stomach. Maybe it was the egg.

"Things out the ordinary, uncommon behavior, for example," she trailed off. His stomach churned again; he looked at his yolk smeared plate. *Definitely the eggs.* "It's L.A.; weird things happen here all the time."

"I know, not much to go on," she said with a shrug.

"I wouldn't even have a clue where or how to start," he said, shaking his head as he finished his coffee.

"I know." She pushed away her plate, "Now you know why I've been so busy and probably look so tired."

"Tired? You look great, not tired at all," Paul said. "In fact you're prettier than I . . ." he faltered, feeling his face start to flush again.

Rie said, chasing away the odd feeling in his stomach, "Thank you, but I feel tired."

"Why didn't you say so? We could have done this another day. You could have gone home to sleep instead."

"Well, I did need to eat, and well, I wanted to see you," she said simply.

"More coffee, dears?"

Candy's voice startled them both.

"No, thank you," Paul said tossing his napkin on his plate. "I'm done."

Rie shook her head as Candy picked up the dirty plates. "I'm finished as well, thank you."

"I'll bring your bill, but no rush; we're not busy at all," Candy said.

"Thanks Candy," Paul said as Candy walked away, then he turned back to Rie. "I'm glad. I really wanted to see you, too."

She smiled back at him making his stomach do cartwheels. Ok, maybe it wasn't just the eggs. He used drinking the last of his water as an excuse to look away from her eyes, their golden flecks utterly captivating. He looked up and saw Candy approaching with the bill and had a thought.

"What's that?" Paul said, pointing out the window.

"What? Where?"

She turned back. Then she saw the bill in his hand.

"Hey . . ." she started.

"Hey, silly, I know, but it worked. It's my treat. I still owe you for saving my life, and it's the least I can do for you coming out for breakfast with me when you're so tired."

"I'm not used to letting people pay for me," she said. "Thank you, I guess."

"You are very welcome," he said, dropping cash on top of the bill. "Did you need to head home or did you want to walk a bit?"

"I'm not ready to go home yet. What did you have in mind?" she asked as they stood up.

"I'm not sure. We'll figure something out."

"You two enjoy the day," Candy said as she swept by with some menus. "Thanks for coming in."

"Thanks, Candy, you have a wonderful day." Paul said opening and holding the door for Rie to step through. "We can grab a cab and head to the stadium; I think there might be a practice. Or head to the Santa Monica Pier?"

"Let's do the pier; I'm not a huge fan of baseball. Plus, walking around will help keep us awake."

"Sounds great," Paul said, pleased at the thought of spending the day with Rie as he hailed a cab.

CHAPTER FOURTEEN

The sun was bright on the weathered planks of the boardwalk as they stepped from the cab. Rie closed her eyes and breathed deep, tasting the salt carried by the slight breeze coming off the ocean as Paul surveyed the people around them. He seemed very comfortable, confident, and at ease, something she never was in large crowds. She remembered her thought from earlier. *Weird or uncommon behavior.* That did seem to surround Paul. People had an odd reaction to him, accepting him immediately, eager for his approval. The incidents at the coffee shop the other day and at breakfast this morning were definitely not regular behavior.

He caught her gaze, a happy grin spreading across his face and, taking her hand, he led her into the crowd. She was torn, let the thought go or pursue it. Thinking of digging into the oddity that seemed to follow Paul made her stomach churn. *Surely, you deserve a day to yourself. Just relax and let it go. Tomorrow is soon enough.* She smiled back at him and followed him into the mass of people.

"Do you like ice cream? It's perfect ice cream weather, not too hot but not too cool."

She couldn't help but shake her head at his childlike enthusiasm as she followed, hyper-aware of the warmth of his hand around hers.

He weaved his way through the crush of people, all eager to enjoy the beautiful day, keeping up a constant chatter.

"I come here every couple of weeks. I love it here. The people, the sound of the ocean, the little market stands, everything."

"This is my first time," Rie managed to say as he pulled her along.

That stopped him in his tracks as he turned to her, eyes wide and mouth open feigning shock. "You've never been here?"

She laughed at his expression and shook her head. "Nope, never been down here before."

"Then you're in for a treat." Paul put his arm around her shoulders and started pointing out different booths and landmarks as they made their way for ice cream.

"They have so many different things, all the things you'd expect in an amusement park really; it just so happens it's on a pier. The typical food carts, restaurants, and rides," he said, excitement filling his voice. "They have rides, too. The Ferris wheel is a landmark, but they also have a roller coaster. There are a couple others, but those two, I like the best."

"I've never really been on any rides, though the Ferris wheel seems like it would be fun." Rie felt herself caught up in Paul's excitement.

"Then we'll have to come back on a night neither of us work because it is absolutely amazing at night."

She nodded, aware of the thrill the thought sent down her back. "I'd like that."

"They have several street artists, too; some of them are very talented. I've bought a couple pieces of spray paint art."

"Really? I've seen people selling that kind of thing but I've never stopped and watched them."

"It's quite interesting. It's amazing what they can do with a couple cans of paint and some paper. We'll pass by as we walk and we can stop for a bit if Tim's here today."

His smile caused another quiver and she had to tear her gaze from his eyes.

"Since it's your first time here, maybe we should just make our way down the pier and get ice cream at the end. Then we can sit and look at the ocean. How does that sound?"

"It's your tour," she said, sweeping her hair over her ear.

She shivered as he grinned at her again and let him take her hand. He led her further down the pier, the heat of the sun tempered by scattered clouds and a cool breeze blowing off the ocean. As they worked through the midmorning crowd, Rie noticed something odd, or at least odd for Los Angeles. Paul, even while he was describing the various types of stores, vendor carts and sights of the pier, was smiling and nodding at the people they passed, occasionally greeting them with a "Hi." That, in itself, was rather different behavior from her experience of L.A., and most other places she had lived.

The really strange part was that people responded with smiles and nods, even the odd wink from a smiling senior or a young woman. Rie had observed life in the bigger cities. Los Angeles, Houston, and especially New York had been full of self-involvement and self-interest, which rarely included consideration for others. Manners and politeness to strangers was not something she saw very often and it definitely made Paul stand out.

And he doesn't even realize it. Rie watched as a man, who a moment ago had scowled at someone brushing by him, smiled and nodded in response to Paul. *He doesn't see how odd this behavior is. It's normal for him. People are responding to him and he doesn't realize how rare that is.*

She turned and looked back. Paul's behavior seemed to be contagious, judging from what she could see in their wake. It was a strange thing to see, almost like night and day: the blank, guarded expressions on the people in front of them against the open and happy ones of those behind.

"Thank you for bringing me here," Rie said impulsively, squeezing his hand, ignoring the way her heart fluttered when Paul turned to her.

"Thank you for coming with me and letting me share it with you," he said. "Oh! Do you like games?"

A laugh broke free at his sudden exuberance as he pulled her toward a game booth.

"The ring toss and darts are fun but they also have a whack-a-mole and a bean bag game. I'm not so good at throwing the bean bags, and I feel kinda silly whacking the mole's heads with the big mallet," he explained as they approached the counter.

"Have you ever played ring toss?" he asked, handing over a couple of bills from his wallet to the sullen teen behind the counter.

"Nope, I can't say that I have," Rie said, as the boy gave Paul the rings.

"It can be a lotta fun. I have good days and bad days. Some days I can't miss, it seems."

They both watched as his first toss hit the lip of a bottle and bounced to the ground. She crooked an eyebrow.

"And other days I couldn't ring a bottle if my life depended on it." His second toss bounced away as well.

A rather sheepish grin spread on his face prompting her to lay her hand on his shoulder, "You just need to relax."

The twinkle in his eyes took her breath away. This guy—what is it about him that makes me feel so warm?

Without looking away from her, he casually tossed the final ring. The distinctive sound it made as it slipped around the neck of a bottle and spun drew both their eyes.

"A winner," the bored teenager said with little enthusiasm, barely paying attention, intent on his smart phone. "You can choose any one of these."

"I can't believe you just did that!" Rie said. Paul's casual shrug made her laugh. "You won big."

He grinned and motioned toward the rather droopy stuffed animals hanging from the ceiling, "No, you have. Pick one. But you have to carry it around."

106

Rie laughed again and pointed at a sad lion in the back row. "I'll take the lion then."

Paul turned to the boy. "She'd like the lion at the back, please."

The teenager didn't even look up as he got off his stool and walked to the back, grabbing a long broomstick as he went. He hooked the lion, catching it with one hand as he carelessly dropped the stick to the floor with a clatter. Rie couldn't help thinking what a contrast his casual rudeness was to the people they'd encountered this morning.

"Here you are . . ." he said trailing off as he looked up for the first time, his eyes catching Paul's calm gaze.

"Thank you very much," Paul said, taking the lion from the boy. "Have a great morning."

"I will, thank you." The boy's smile seemed to signal a drastic change in attitude, "You too."

The teen's change really struck Rie and started nagging at the back of her mind as Paul, with a grandiose flourish, presented her with the lion. "Your prize."

"Why, thank you," she said with a slight bow.

"Bye!" The boy called to them as they walked away.

Paul waved back as Rie snuggled her hand in his arm, hanging the lion in the crook of the other, "Do they have cotton candy? I used to love cotton candy."

"They do. We can get some from a cart just down the way," Paul said, pointing down the boardwalk.

"Then let's go!" Rie tugged on his arm, pulling her mind back and shoving the concerns away. *Just let go and enjoy the day.*

She delighted in Paul's laugh as they walked arm in arm down the boardwalk, people smiling in their wake, the sound of their footsteps lost in the bustle around them. Paul continued to talk about the pier, the different things he had seen during his many visits to the boardwalk, and made her laugh with his descriptions of the characters.

In the midst of a describing an extremely colorful vendor, she felt his arm tense and she glanced around to see what had caught his attention. Rie noticed the crowd in front of them parting around a game, voices raised in anger, obviously arguing over something. She started to slow down, searching for a different direction to walk. Paul absently patted her arm, his attention focused on the conflict ahead of them as he pulled her onward.

A few steps away, he released her arm and motioned her to stop as he continued on. The crowd around them sounded loud and harsh, faces tight as they called out insults toward the vendor or customer, depending on their individual views. From where she stood, Rie could tell the argument was between the stall vendor and another man, the narrow shelf between them the only barrier keeping the argument from escalating to violence. Noticing the clenched fists of the tall customer, Rie wasn't sure how much longer it would remain so.

"Don't try to cheat me!"

"I'm not cheating nobody, them's the rules! Three darts, three throws. Three balloons gets you a prize," the vendor said defiantly, shaking a handful of darts at the angry customer.

"And I hit all three! You saw it! Your stupid, dull darts can't even pop a simple balloon!"

The customer's angry response brought a cheer from the crowd and an almost equal amount of boos. The crowd was pretty evenly mixed between supporters and Rie hoped it wouldn't turn ugly.

"Hold on guys. Surely, it can't be so important to bring you both to such a heated argument," Paul said, his calm and quiet tone drawing the attention of both men.

Rie watched both turn and focus on him even as the itch in the back of her head, the trail of thought she had been ignoring all morning, started tickling again when the crowd slowly started to quiet down. Both men turned to Paul, as if to an impartial judge. The noise of the crowd disappeared as the angry customer appealed to Paul.

"It's simple. He's cheating me," the tall man responded, shaking his fist at the vendor.

"Wait, wait, please," Paul interrupted holding his hands up. "Can I get your names?"

"Joe," the customer said curtly, crossing his arms and glaring at the vendor.

"My name is Chris, and I ain't cheating him. The rules are the rules."

"It has nothing to do with the rules!" Joe yelled slamming his hand on the counter, "It's about those crappy darts that can't even pop a balloon!"

Paul held up his hand interrupting Chris's response as he laid his other hand on Joe's shoulder. "Easy, no need to yell, my friend. May I see the darts?" Paul asked.

"Five dollars to play," Chris said shoving his hand at Paul, a scowl distorting his face.

"I have no intention of playing, but if it will help resolve this, here." Paul handed over a five dollar bill and kept his hand out, waiting for the darts.

Chris looked from Paul to Joe and then, shaking his head, laid three darts in Paul's outstretched hand. "Fine. But there ain't nuthin' wrong with them darts."

"May I see the darts Joe threw, please," Paul asked, laying the darts down on the counter.

Chris bent and picked up a dart lying on the ground near the back wall. He tossed the dart onto the counter beside the three darts already there.

Rie watched Paul pick up two darts and hold them up together. She couldn't see anything different from where she stood and, sensing the threat of violence had passed for the moment, stepped up beside Paul. She saw one dart, the dart from the ground, had a noticeably bent and dull tip. One of the two darts still on the counter displayed the same type of damage. By Paul's stance, she could tell he had noticed the same thing.

"It appears this dart is ruined, as is this one," he said holding up the bent dart and then scooping up the other from the counter. "It is unfortunate the damage escaped your notice. Personally, I think it would be fair to let Joe re-throw his third dart, using a good one."

Paul set the defective darts off to the side and Rie watched as Chris looked back and forth between Paul and the two flawed darts. The crowd around them hummed with murmured conversation as they realized what Paul had noticed. Chris appeared like he was going to refuse when Paul reached and laid his hand on his shoulder.

"Please, my friend, it would be the fair thing to do and would resolve this conflict easily."

"I . . ." Chris started to reply and paused, his attention on Paul.

Rie peered around her. The entire crowd seemed focused on the three men in front of her. Gone were jeering faces, eager to see a fight. Everyone seemed calm, taking in the scene before them, patiently waiting for the outcome. Her gaze fixed on the three men, she waited with the crowd.

"I guess that would be fair," Chris finally said. "In fact, he can use a brand new dart."

A large smile spread across Paul's face as Chris set down an unopened box of darts in front of Joe. "Thank you. There you are, Joe, that's fair, I think."

The stern expression left Joe's face as he opened the box and picked out a dart. "It is very fair, thank you."

"I'm glad we could sort this out. Throw whenever you're ready."

Paul's speech turned casual, the vendor stepping to the side, as Joe finished assembling the dart. Rie held her breath with the crowd around them as Joe stepped to the counter and took aim. She saw the calm on Paul's faced and marveled at the ease with which he had prevented a potentially violent argument. She let her eyes roam across his face, free for the first time to really focus on him, the way his eyes sparkled, the curve of his lips, the way his hair fell across his forehead.

She was so engrossed she didn't even notice when Joe threw, she only heard the crowd gasp and a loud POP! Followed by a loud cheer. Rie turned and saw the ragged pieces of the pierced balloon flutter in the ocean breeze.

"Well done!" Paul cried, clapping Joe on the shoulder. "What has my friend here won?"

"That makes three balloons popped; he gets his choice of prizes." Chris waved at the shelves behind him.

"Thank you for your help," Joe said, turning to Paul. "I don't even know your name."

"Ah, my name is Paul. I'm glad I was able to clear things up between the two of you. It's far too nice of a day to fight."

"Yes. Thank you, Paul," the vendor said, holding out his hand.

"You're welcome." Paul shook the proffered hand. "I hope you both have a great rest of your morning."

They both nodded and waved at him as he turned back to Rie.

"I'm sorry about that, but everything is okay now," he said, putting his arm around her. "Now let's see about getting you some cotton candy."

The nagging feeling she was missing something important faded as Rie felt herself relax. She smiled back at him as they made their way through the thinning crowd.

CHAPTER FIFTEEN

"Hi, Rie."

Mkai felt sorry at the way Rie jumped as she stepped in the darkness of the bar.

"Kai! You startled me," she said as she walked over to where he stood.

"It was unfair to greet you so abruptly. I apologize," Mkai said as she peeled off her jacket. *She looks tired.*

"Oh no, it's all right. I just have to check in with Tony. Give me a bit and then come grab a stool."

He watched her walking across the bar, waving at the big man as she went up to him. Mkai glanced around the almost empty bar and, with no patience to wait, followed in her footsteps.

She was talking to Tony as Kai quietly settled on a stool.

"I am really sorry, Tony. I know I'm late," she said as she slipped around the counter and crammed her jacket and purse under the bar.

"Hey, no problem, Rie. The wife can wait a bit for me. It's good for her, once in a while." Tony's big grin made her chuckle.

"Yeah, I'm sure. She's probably glad for some extra peace and quiet," she said as he started for the back.

He just smiled and waved. "Have a good night. The rain's probably gonna make it a slow night, but call me or Rick if you get busy."

"I will, thanks. Have a great evening." Rie waved. "Tell Becca I said 'Hi.'"

Tony disappeared behind the swinging door as she turned and faced Mkai.

"I'm sorry, I'm running late today. I lost track of time or I would have . . ." she started.

"No, no, please, don't concern yourself. You didn't know I would be stopping in today."

"I wish I had good news for you," Rie said, leaning on the bar and lowering her voice, "I talked to everyone I know and none of them have heard anything unusual. But they will keep an eye out for me.""I don't have to ask, but I hope you were circumspect about it?" he said.

"Of course. Not only because half wouldn't understand what I was getting at but also because I wanted to make sure not to attract any notice." She handed him his regular drink.

"I am glad to hear that." Mkai took a small sip and grimaced at the harsh taste. "It may take days before we hear anything so you may have to keep checking with them."

"You know, I've always wondered why you drink that vile stuff," she said.

He looked at the glass of bitter liquor and then looked up at her. His mind went back to the first taste of the Malört in Chicago decades before. *It was as bitter then as it is now and, as always, reminds me of the bitter taste of Hell.*

"It's not a big deal, I've been drinking it for years." he said, picking up the glass and swirling it around. "Have you ever tried it?"

"I tried once, when you first asked me about ordering a bottle for you."

"And?" he asked with a grin, knowing the answer.

"I thought my face was going to fall off, it was so bitter," she said, laughing.

"Yeah, that's exactly what I thought the first time I tasted it." He took another sip, tongue curling as it always did. "It is a remembrance of Hell, not that I need one. And it makes my senses appreciate the freshness of this world anew each time I drink it."

He could tell his answer wasn't what Rie expected and he was touched by the sympathy and compassion in her eyes when she looked at him.

"I'm sorry, Kai. I can't even begin to understand."

Her casual touch on his hand shook him, more than almost anything else ever had, and he struggled to keep it from his face.

"Thank you, but unnecessary. I will have to get a cell phone so you can contact me when you find out anything."

She looked at him a moment, "That would be good. Time is probably pretty sensitive right now, isn't it?"

"Yes, very much so," he nodded, relieved that she let him change the subject. "Speaking of time, or losing track of it, it is not something I have ever known to happen to you."

"Not my usual, no. I was out . . . with a friend," she said, hiding a yawn behind her hand. "I didn't get much sleep before having to come in for my shift."

The bar was dark, but it wasn't nearly as dark as the depths of Hell so the blush creeping across her cheeks was quite obvious to Mkai. It was obvious as well that, regardless of how close they were, she still felt shy about talking about it.

"A . . . friend? I'm guessing a male friend from the pause. Something else I do not remember as being usual for you. And an important one, if you spent the day with him instead of sleeping."

"Not normal for me, no; it's rather new. We actually only met a couple days ago. His name is Paul. I kinda saved him from being hit by a car," she said, embarrassment obvious in the halting way she spoke.

"You did? That is a great thing." Mkai's lip curved into a smile. "And you're now discovering something between you?"

"Yes, I've been thinking about him . . . a lot. It's not something I can say I've really experienced before," she said.

Mkai was touched and surprised by her honesty. "The circumstances under which you met often do encourage certain feelings, but perhaps you were meant to meet."

"You mean fate? I didn't think you would believe in fate," Rie said, frowning.

"Oh, of course we do. God does exist and He does have a great plan. Certain events are indeed meant to happen. The little details though, the little choices, those are all part of the free will with which He gifted you."

Rie nodded slowly. "It's so strange, but I have felt there was meaning behind us meeting, a reason for it."

"Then please, if you will, tell me about him," Mkai said with a smile. "He sounds like he may be important to you and your future."

"I think so," she began. "He is not like anyone I know. He's kind and nice to everyone. He laughs and smiles a lot." Her struggle to put her feelings about Paul into words was apparent.

"Good qualities, all," Mkai said, sipping from his drink, the bitterness twisting his mouth. "So you were out with him today?"

"Yes, we met for breakfast after work. He works nights as well. Then we walked around awhile; he took me to the pier," Rie said. "He is so much nicer and more open than any guy I've ever met. He says 'hi' to everyone."

"Really? Here, in Los Angeles?" Mkai said.

"I know, so weird right? People react to him. Almost everyone smiles at him and responds to him in some way." Rie reached for a bar rag and started to wipe down the counter.

"That is different, yes. Not as strange as if this was New York, but still rather unique." Mkai chuckled. "It is a special talent."

"He makes me laugh."

"That is a special talent as well," Mkai said.

"I think I've smiled and laughed more today than I have in a long, long time," Rie said, looking at the counter, her finger tracing circles on the bar top.

"Then I am glad, and I hope one day to perhaps meet the man who brings such joy to you."

"I would like that."

Mkai watched Rie glance over as the door opened, flooding the bar with light.

"Well this is your chance," she said, turning to Mkai as a man approached.

"Hi, Rie. I have the night off so I thought I'd come for a beer or two. I hope that's okay?"

She smiled and waved Paul to a stool. The air seemed to vibrate around him and Mkai struggled to contain his shock. *It can't be, not this simple.*

"You mean you're not tired of me yet?" she said as he settled at the bar. "What would you have? We have Bud and Coors on tap."

"Bud is good, thank you." He glanced at Mkai two stools over. "I hope I'm not interrupting anything."

Mkai watched the interaction between the two, the change in Rie quite apparent. The tiredness that had bowed her shoulders and dulled her eyes was gone. She almost bounced where she stood looking at Paul. Her eyes were bright and lively. He looked back and forth between them. It was more than just her interest in Paul that had affected the change. He could almost feel the flow of energy from Paul to Rie.

"Oh, not at all, this is an *old* friend of mine," she said, all trace of sleepiness completely gone. Mkai caught the emphasis and studied Paul for a reaction. "Paul, this is Kai. Kai, this is Paul, who I was just telling you about."

All Paul did was raise an eyebrow slightly while turning to Mkai and sticking out his hand, "Hello Kai, it's a pleasure to meet a friend of Rie's."

"Rie was just telling me how the two of you met. It is my pleasure to meet you as well, Paul," Mkai said with effort, the impact of Paul's touch almost sending him off his stool.

"It was quite the way to meet," Paul chuckled, as Rie passed him a beer, "and then she spent most of day with me. I think to make sure I didn't play in traffic."

Rie shook her head in mock disbelief. "Someone had to keep an eye on you. It would be a rather sad waste to save you one moment only to have you cause a huge accident later."

Paul grinned, "Well I'm glad you did. I had a really good time today. I hope it won't make you too tired for your shift."

"I should be good. I went home and crashed for a couple hours; that's all I really needed," Rie said. "And you? Did you finally get home and get some sleep?"

"Yeah. I just woke up and thought I'd come for a beer since I don't work tonight," he said.

They seem unaware of how they shine together. But Mkai could see it, in the way they leaned toward each other, the smiles lighting their faces. The energy around Paul seemed to stretch out and wrap around Marie, warming the air around the two of them, the connection between them feeding on itself, getting stronger until Mkai could almost see it. He glanced around the bar. He saw only a couple tables of rough looking men sharing a pitcher of beer. No one but him to bear witness. He watched the way Rie leaned toward Paul, completely engrossed in what he was saying. They both seemed oblivious to his presence. A thought crossed his mind.

"Rie, I must leave. We will talk again soon." Mkai interrupted, abruptly standing and gulping his drink, almost choking as the bitterness hit his throat.

He hated leaving so quickly but if he was being followed, they must not enter the bar. Not now. It was obvious in the way Rie looked at him she was confused and perhaps a little hurt at his behavior. It was unfortunate, but Mkai hoped he'd be able to explain it later. He turned to Paul, a shiver racing down his spine.

"Paul, it was a very great pleasure to meet you. I hope to get to know you well."

"Kai, it was nice to meet you as well. Any friend of Rie's is a friend of mine, so I would enjoy that," Paul held out his hand.

Mkai hesitated just a moment, steeling himself before taking Paul's hand.

"Rie, we'll talk soon, I'll probably be back in a couple of days. Until then, be well."

He nodded to them both and hurried from the bar, aware of how odd his behavior must seem to Rie, and likely to Paul. *It can't be helped, you must keep them safe. And you can't do that from here.* Mkai shook his head. He couldn't believe he had to walk away, he had to leave. But it was the only way to keep the two of them safe.

CHAPTER SIXTEEN

Mkai stopped and took a deep breath as the door slowly closed behind him. He couldn't afford to stay in this area too long. He couldn't risk drawing attention to Rie and Paul. Especially if his suspicions were correct. He had barely been able to contain the shock when he first touched Paul's hand. Even after this long, there was no mistaking the feel of God.

The easy, casual banter between the two was not something he had ever seen Rie do. She had always kept herself at a distance. He didn't think she even realized it but, with Paul, her defenses were down completely.

That is the real Marie, not the Rie persona she's hidden behind for so long. Combine that with what I felt shaking Paul's hand, and yes, there is something about him. Hurry As'hame, you're the only one who can tell for sure.

If he was being followed he didn't want to draw any attention to Rie or Paul. He really didn't like leaving the two of them without protection but his presence would be more likely to draw attention than anything else. It was a complete accident that he had discovered Paul. Chances were good he, they, would be safe.

You yourself didn't feel or sense anything until you were feet away from him, and that's not likely to happen. The best way to keep them safe is to not draw attention to them.

His mind whirled as he walked. He couldn't believe the odds of finding Paul the way Rie did. He still needed As'hame to verify, but Mkai was almost positive Paul was the man they were searching for. Now the two of them just had to stay safe until As'hame returned. Mkai decided if he had to wander he might as well head back to where he first talked to As'hame. It was as good a place as any. He hurried through the early evening, never noticing the shadowy form leaping from rooftop to rooftop behind him.

Mkai climbed the fire escape as full darkness cloaked the city. Regardless of whether As'hame arrived soon or not, he would have to do something. They couldn't afford to wait too long. But what to do? He knew Roger would have the equipment ready by tomorrow but would check in anyway. How to get Rie and Paul somewhere safe without the wrong people noticing and without either of them freaking out?

Mkai stepped to the edge of the roof and glanced once more to the east, the direction from which As'hame would arrive. Nothing. He had to return soon. Time was critical. Mkai heard a furtive noise from behind. He whirled around drawing the dagger from his belt. The snarl on the demon's face showed its anger as it burst from behind the stairwell and charged. Mkai leapt forward and, at the last second, pivoted on his front leg, letting the demon slide by. He plunged his dagger in its scaled back, allowing the thrust to turn him to face his enemy.

The fiend stumbled and reached a claw to its back, a snarled scream barely restrained from bursting out. Mkai charged back in and, ducking under an outstretched arm, slammed in shoulder first. He heard a rib snap as the brute was crushed back against the stairs and fell to its knees with a gasp. *I guess watching all the NFL really paid off.*

Mkai stepped forward drawing the Ar'kt dagger and squatted before his foe.

"I don't recognize you, which is unfortunate for you," he said, slowly dragging the Ar'kt across the dagger's blade, the scattering sparks drawing the other's eyes. "Either way, you're not leaving this rooftop alive, but it might have saved you some pain."

Mkai waited until the demon glared at him, agony filling its slitted eyes, "Why are . . ." it started to snarl.

It cut off abruptly as Mkai thrust the Ar'kt, stopping a hair's breadth from its eye. "Answer only what I ask you; otherwise, stay silent. You are following me. I want to know why." Mkai thought he already knew, but he had to go through the motions in case there was another watcher.

"Word came down that you turned traitor. Not only are you associating with the damned As'rai but you've killed your own kind!" said the fiend, fangs bared in hate.

"Who have I killed?" Mkai said.

"Well, it's assumed you killed Rahale and the others. They never returned from hunting you."

"Ah, well now. That I did do. I killed them. All three." He paused. "With this, the Ar'kt dagger," he continued, holding the blade up and slowly turning it in the fading light.

"That's it! Take him!" The shout coming from behind startled him.

With a sinking heart Mkai thrust the Ar'kt dagger home in the demon's chest. Mkai twisted the dagger and pulled it free, wrenching a howl from the demon as it convulsed once and died. He stood and turned with his back toward a door to the stairs. He stood defiant, drew his second dagger, and stood with a blade in each hand. He watched as first one, and then another and another demon crawled over the side of the roof. They gathered until there were six facing him, identical snarls on their scaled faces. He shrugged his shoulders and waited for them to rush him. But they stood silent and still, in a line, waiting.

"What are you waiting for? Come on!"

"They are waiting for me, for I have claimed you." The raspy drawl sent chills down Mkai's spine.

He struggled to hide his shock as yet one more form slipped onto the roof and slowly stood. Drekor. It was worse than Mkai thought. He hadn't expected to win against three but had emerged victorious. There was the slightest sliver of hope against six on the narrow roof top. He had none against Drekor.

There was no mistaking what stood before him. A creature of nightmares. Created and given form from the depths of the most vile and twisted mind. Brought forth to torment and kill all who crossed her path. She towered over the fiends crouched at her cloven feet. Ridges and spikes jutting from arms and shoulders glistened black in the faint light, madness filling her blood red eyes. Mkai's skin crawled as it always did when he was near her. Most of the fallen had been cursed by God for their choice. Scales and horns replaced glistening wings; they were allowed to keep a human form but a distorted caricature of it. But some demons, at the beginning of the war, had chosen forms of terror. They had distanced themselves from the sanctity of God, and these God punished most severely. The forms they chose became the forms they were stuck in for all eternity. And then they were kicked from Heaven, their powers and abilities stripped from them, and were sent crashing into the depths of Hell, bound to never return.

The banishment from Heaven, her choice of form now permanent, had only hastened Drekor's descent into cruelty and insanity. She relished the fear she evoked in human and demon alike. She existed only to kill, in the most gruesome and painful ways possible. He stood alone against her and, Ar'kt dagger or not, he knew had no chance.

"The Mistress sent me for you. Long have you been watched, you who shun your brothers, who keep this misguided glamour when walking amongst the filth of mankind." She rasped, her forked tongue flickering in the light.

"Even now, knowing your true form is visible to us as we stand here, you insist on keeping the charade. It is lucky for you that she wants you alive, or at least somewhat."

Mkai felt a chill as she smirked at him, fanged mouth gaping wide, "But she said I could play first."

Mkai fought the quiver in his hands. The nightmarish form started toward him and Mkai struggled to remain calm. His mind raced through options. He had no chance facing her head on. He spared a glance at the edge but despaired, knowing the fall wasn't high enough to kill him. It would only cripple him and delay the inevitable. He glanced at the dagger. Taking his own life was still something not allowed to him.

Another gift left to us from God. To not harm ourselves, to ensure we lived to regret turning our backs on Him. He steeled himself for the likely short fight before him.

"Then what are you waiting for? Alone, I may be, but fear of you has long left me," Mkai said. "And taking me alive is simply not a choice I will leave you."

"We shall see."

"Alone, you are not!" The power of the shout from above stopped them and all eyes looked up in unison.

Mkai smiled in relief and surprise as first one, then another and one more sunlit form dropped onto the roof between him and the towering menace of Drekor.

"She is mine." The quiet resolution in Ro'molr's voice was enough for As'hame and Ti'raon to move to the side, leaving him space as he walked forward.

"Ro'molr," Drekor snarled, clenching claw tipped hands.

"I warned you last time we met that if you visited this plane again it would be for the last time." The sharp sound of a sword being drawn filled the air. "I keep my word."

Ro'molr barely finished when Drekor leapt forward. Her speed was almost a fatal surprise as Ro'molr ducked to the side and rolled out of the way. Mkai watched as Ro'molr kept rolling, trying to get to his feet as she leapt at him again. He managed to get to one knee and was barely able to deflect her killing stroke with his blade. He kicked out with a booted foot, knocking her back, and stood.

"You are not as invincible as you may believe," Drekor growled and struck out so fast she appeared like a blur to Mkai's eyes.

Ro'molr retreated from the onslaught as she moved him backward across the roof. Mkai couldn't understand what he was seeing. Drekor was more than most demons, stronger and faster. But she was nothing compared to an angel. Banished from Heaven or not, the As'rai were angels. Regardless of her speed, her power and her size, when faced by even the lowest angel, her defeat should have been a foregone conclusion. He couldn't understand why Ro'molr seemed to be struggling.

Ro'molr dodged another charge, his return blow glancing off the scales protecting her arms. Ro'molr backpedaled, blade held in front him as Drekor stalked across the roof. Ro'molr kept feinting and dodging, drawing her after him step by step. Mkai finally realized what he was witnessing.

"As'rai!" the cry burst forth, stilling everything on the roof.

Mkai watched as first Ti'raon and then As'hame charged around the two battling in the center of the roof. A ruse. It had all been a ruse to separate her from the other demons. Demons that were now alone.

"She is yours, Ro'molr. We will take care of the rabble." Ti'raon's clear voice rang out as she and As'hame rushed around the edge of the roof.

Ro'molr gave an answering grin without taking his gaze from his foe. "It's been long in coming, Drekor, but tonight, it ends."

"As'rai!" Ro'molr lifted his blade to the sky as he gave voice to the war cry of his order.

Drekor howled and leapt at the angel advancing toward her. Ro'molr struck with his sword, blood spraying the air, even as he ducked and rolled under her charge. He spun back to his feet as she whirled to face him, the green ichor of her blood dripping from the wound in her side. She put a clawed hand to her side then lifted it to her face, blood staining her palm. Mkai grimaced in disgust as her forked tongue lapped at her hand. Ro'molr stood watching her calmly, waiting for her next charge. She gathered herself even as the clash of battle came to them.

Mkai watched in awe as As'hame and Ti'raon crashed into the group of demons. His heart soared as he saw the angels battling before him. The demons fell back into one another, jostling and shoving, trying to stay clear of the attacking angels. Their cries of fear filled the air as Ro'molr went on the offensive and attacked, blade against claw. The fight was brutal. There was no room for careful planning or artful dodging, no mercy to be had.

With every swing of Ro'molr's sword, Drekor was forced back. She struggled to block and divert his blade and Mkai rejoiced to see the look of fear cross her face. As'hame and Ti'raon were making short work of the demons, with three already down. *Make that four.* Ti'raon grabbed an outstretched claw and slammed her blade into the owner's chest. He watched as she spun, hauled the demon with her and, with a heave, flung it off the roof, blood trailing free.

With a cry of hate, Drekor leapt forward, clawed hands sweeping down. Ro'molr dropped and rolled to his knees behind her and with a blurring stroke cut back and across. Drekor screamed as his blade hit her cleanly for the first time. The sound of ribs breaking was audible even through the raging battle on the rooftop. She fell to her back, cloven feet pushing, struggling for traction on the blood slick roof. She crawled backward away from Ro'molr as he slowly advanced, ichor staining his blade.

The last pair fell to Ti'raon and As'hame with almost identical moves and the two angels turned to watch Ro'molr. Drekor barred her fangs in final defiance as he lifted his blade. He raised it to the sky and paused, the last of the light making it shine softly.

"It is over, Drekor. Finally, your tormented existence has come to an end," Ro'molr said. "I cannot forgive you for all that you have done, but I can hope you find rest."

"My death doesn't matter," Drekor rasped, pain thick in her voice, "you will still lose."

"We are the As'rai," As'hame said, joining his friend. "We do not lose." Mkai thrilled at those words, amid sadness that he was and always would be an outsider to their order.

"Fools!" she howled, and then gasped as Ro'molr sunk his blade into her chest.

A claw grasped it weakly and, for a moment, the madness fled from Drekor's eyes. Blood filled her mouth as the angel twisted and pulled his sword free. She slowly slumped sideways, a small smile, almost of relief, forming on her crooked, fang-filled mouth. The mad light in her eyes faded and her last breath rattled free.

"It's over," Ro'molr said in a quiet whisper.

"They are avenged," As'hame said, putting his hand on his friend's shoulder. "The souls of Abydos can rest now."

Mkai looked at As'hame as Ro'molr stared down at his foe, anger tight across his face.

"It was a city that Drekor single-handedly destroyed," As'hame answered Mkai's unspoken question.

"The city was under my protection and, when I was called away by the Council, she slaughtered the inhabitants. They died because I wasn't there," Ro'molr said, anger harsh in his voice.

"And she paid for her actions tonight," Ti'raon said, "We are free to search for Him now."

"There's no need for that," Mkai interjected, holding up his hand, sirens screaming in the distance, getting closer with each moment.

He halted as three pairs of crystal clear eyes, one green and two blue turned from watching Drekor's body fade to focus on him.

He waited a heartbeat.

"I think I've found Him."

CHAPTER SEVENTEEN

As'hame's boots thudded on his balcony, closely followed by Ti'raon. Ro'molr and Mkai swept in, Mkai almost stumbling as Ro'molr let him go. Ro'molr steadied him and then clapped him on the shoulder, hard.

"See, that wasn't too bad," Ro'molr said as Mkai stumbled again.

As'hame opened the balcony door with a wry shake of his head. *Ro'molr never could be serious for too long.* They filed past As'hame as he ushered them into his apartment. Ro'molr sauntered to the kitchen as Ti'raon went to the large window overlooking the bay. Mkai moved unsteadily to the couch and sat down, obviously still shaken from the flight. *It is no wonder, with Ro'molr pretending to drop him twice.* As'hame glanced around his apartment. Until now, no one had set foot in his sanctuary other than him. And now, there were three. He looked around again, slightly curious about their reactions. He had put a lot of thought into his sanctuary. A large flat screen TV hung on one wall with an elaborate entertainment system on a low table below it. He'd hung abstract paintings on another wall. He wondered if anyone would recognize them as originals. The third wall was taken up by shelves filled with books and odds and ends. There was a large, overstuffed sofa and several comfortable chairs scattered around.

"You have quite an interesting collection," Mkai said. "A goblet, ancient Roman by the looks of it. Is that a dagger from the Tang dynasty?"

"Thank you. Yes, I have collected something from every place and time I have ever been. There are shards of pottery from Babylon, a collection of arrowheads from Egypt, even a Mayan Pitz ball."

"You have been watching humans for a long time. This can't be everything." Mkai said, as Ti'raon wandered back toward them.

"No, it is not. Some I have in storage, some I have arranged to be discovered by man, and some have been left behind or destroyed. We are not infallible, and the forces of nature can overwhelm us, as well," As'hame said, sadness washing over him.

"He was at Pompeii when that city was destroyed," Ti'raon said.

As'hame stepped over to the shelves. "I was. And could do nothing. I fled the city, barely keeping ahead of the cloud of ash that covered her people. Their screams haunt me at times."

He picked up a piece of stone, half the size of his fist. He turned it over to reveal the faded color of a mosaic, surprisingly bright after two thousand years.

"There was nothing you could do As'hame. We share your grief over its loss," Ti'raon said, offering up the support he had come to depend on from her.

"It is an old loss, but time does not lessen it." He placed the piece of wall from his lost city back in its spot.

"You love them, don't you?"

Mkai's question surprised As'hame for a moment and then he smiled.

"Yes, I do. I have watched them living in the smallest, mud huts to the largest, sprawling cities, with always the same struggle to live." As'hame paused. "If anything, it is their struggle to live, their passion, which draws me to them."

"It's that empathy, your understanding of them, which makes you the greatest of us," Ro'molr said as he came from the kitchen with a beer in one hand, a pickle in the other.

Ro'molr dropped beside Mkai and stretched out his now bare feet. The burly angel sighed as he took a drink from the bottle.

"Oh, I took your last beer," he said, raising the bottle in a toast.

As'hame laughed. "I may have empathy and a certain understanding of humans but, you, my friend, are almost one of them."

"Bad habits and all," Ti'raon said with a grin, nudging his legs as she moved to the other of side Mkai.

As'hame caught Mkai's eye as they listened to the banter between the two. Mkai nodded.

"Mkai, are you ready to explain your statement of earlier?"

As'hame's quiet words brought an instant silence as all eyes turned to him.

"Yes. By rather a lucky coincidence, I think I have found the man we seek."

"How?" Ti'raon asked leaning forward.

"I have only two contacts left alive in this city," Mkai began.

"Alive?" Ro'molr interrupted.

"Yes. I had been watched at our first meeting and after fighting and defeating Rahale, they sent Drekor. She killed all but two they didn't know about."

"Then they are avenged as well," Ro'molr said with an air of satisfaction.

"They are, indeed. That was well done," As'hame said, and motioned Mkai to continue.

"One, Roger, is collecting everything I could think we might need, though I think now we may need two vehicles. My second contact, Rie, gathers information. I have told them both about us and who we are and what we are trying to do."

"What!" Ti'raon said, "How could you share such information with them? That could put the whole search in jeopardy."

As'hame said, "I agreed with his reasoning. They are risking a lot for us and deserve to know." He smiled at Mkai, "And who knows, they will likely work harder knowing what is at stake."

"I couldn't let them risk so much without knowing. Roger believes and wants to do whatever he can to help. Rie . . . Marie is a different story. She's an atheist but, as she pointed out, she doesn't need to believe in order to help. Though I think she is more open now than she was."

Ti'raon shook her head. "I know that there are many who do not believe. Their understanding of science clouds their faith. They cannot see a way to combine the two, thinking them contradictions. But I cannot understand how they can view their world, the beauty of the universe around us and not believe in the touch of the Divine."

"I think, before this is through, she may change her view," As'hame said.

Mkai continued. "I waited a couple of days to give her time and then met her at her work. She works at a local bar. While I was there, he came in."

"Just like that?" Ti'raon asked, looking at As'hame. "This cannot be a happenstance."

"His name is Paul. They met only a few days ago and spent the morning together. I only stayed long enough to be sure of what I felt when I met him," Mkai said. "I didn't want to stay long in case I was being followed again."

"Good thinking." Ro'molr nodded in approval.

"I wandered around a while so the bar wouldn't stand out and then went to where As'hame and I first spoke."

"I am not sure if there is Divine Will happening here or it is just a fateful coincidence, though I know which I am leaning toward. Regardless, it has definitely improved the situation," As'hame said.

"Mkai, when I left, it was to inform the As'rai and appeal for their aid. Ti'raon and Ro'molr are here, for a start, but more will be arriving."

"Soon, I hope."

"Yes, I asked the Council to send them as they arrived. The quicker we get reinforcements, even one at a time, the better." As'hame sighed. "I doubt we will have time to wait for a sizable force to gather before they will be needed."

"So the Council agreed to help?" Mkai asked.

"More than just help. They are calling As'rai from around the world. Every As'rai that can be spared is gathering for this."

"Then we have a chance."

"One which should not be risked." Ti'raon said, leaning forward, "Where is He? We must get to Him."

"Ti'raon was there, the first time." As'hame said to Mkai.

She reminded As'hame of a bird of prey, a falcon focused on her target. She would allow nothing to stop her from what she saw as her duty.

"I will not let it happen again," Ti'raon said. "I will keep Him safe this time."

"I don't know where He lives, or anything more than His name. But Rie will." Mkai stood. "She is still at work. We can see her at the bar."

"Then what?" Ro'molr asked.

"Then comes the hard part." As'hame paused. "We convince Him."

"Then what are we waiting for? Let's go," Ti'raon said, standing and moving toward the door.

"Can we fly again?" Mkai asked, excitement flooding his face, at odds with the scales and horns of his form.

"Yes, we do not have time to waste." As'hame said smiling at his exuberance. "Ro'molr."

"What! Oh man, not again," Ro'molr said, shaking his head with mock dismay. "Why do I always have to carry him?"

"Well, I guess . . ." Mkai started to say, disappointment apparent in his voice and manner.

"Ignore him, Mkai," Ti'raon interrupted. "He thinks he is funny."

Ro'molr laughed and clapped Mkai on the shoulder and led him toward the balcony. "Don't worry Mkai, I won't drop you. Honest."

As'hame smiled to himself at the way his two oldest friends accepted Mkai. Including him in their ages long banter was unexpected. *But not too surprising. They know how important this is. And we need all the allies we can get.*

He followed the three to the balcony, taking a moment to look around. *You might not be back for a while. If ever.* Sadness touched him briefly before he was able to shake it off. *This is what we were made for, everything has built to this. We cannot fail.*

A sudden shout spoke of Ro'molr surprising Mkai and As'hame hurried through the door. Ti'raon shook her head with mock disdain when he joined her on the balcony.

"He is such a child. He dragged Mkai onto the rail, and then shoved him off. That was the shout."

As'hame didn't fight the laugh bursting out at the image and, after a moment, Ti'raon joined him. Her crystal laugh shone in his heart as it always did and, with a grateful wink, he leapt into the air, winging toward Ro'molr's distant silhouette. He heard the beat of Ti'raon's wings and knew she was following close behind. As he caught up to Ro'molr he could make out Mkai pointing and giving directions from where he hung in Ro'molr's grip.

"About two more blocks and then right a couple more and we can set down in the alley."

"Two more blocks and right?" Ro'molr asked, letting go of one arm and pointing.

As'hame could see the big grin on his face when Mkai shouted and flailed.

"Yes! Now grab my arm!" Mkai cried, hanging on desperately.

There was no disguising the fear lacing his voice and As'hame signaled Ro'molr with nod of his head. Ro'molr grinned back and heaved on Mkai, catching his free hand.

"Stop doing that!" Mkai said as he hung from Ro'molr's grip.

"Stop doing what?" Ro'molr asked shrugging his shoulders, rocking Mkai.

"That! Stop almost dropping me. Please."

"Oh, that? Sure. Why didn't you say something?"

As'hame glanced past Ro'molr to Ti'raon and smiled. It lifted his heart to be with his friends once more. *How can we lose?*

Mkai signaled and As'hame followed Ro'molr as he banked and glided into the alley Mkai pointed out. If they could get to Paul first and keep Him safe, then there really was hope.

CHAPTER EIGHTEEN

"Rie."

She looked up in surprise as Mkai stepped up to the bar. "Kai! I didn't expect to see you for a couple of days."

"I know. That's actually why I'm here." He leaned forward and nodded his head at the door to the back. "Can we go out back for a moment?"

She glanced around the almost empty bar, "Yeah, Joe and Theo are both regulars, they'll be fine for a bit. Just give me a minute."

He nodded in relief as she walked over to the two men sitting at the bar. She talked with them for a moment until one burst out laughing and they both nodded at her. They moved their chairs around so they both could see the door and went back to their beer. He smiled, watching as she laughed and shook her finger at one and then walked back toward him.

"We're good. I told them they'd get a free round if they'll watch the bar and come get me if anyone comes in."

"Excellent. Thank you. I wouldn't normally ask you to do this but it's very important," Mkai said, ushering her toward the back. "Hopefully it won't take long."

Rie paused as she stepped into the gloom of the alley, evidently surprised at the three shadows standing silently by the door. She looked to Mkai, slight concern in her eyes.

Here we go. "Don't worry, these are friends." Mkai loved the way it felt to address the angels so.

"You have nothing to fear, we are indeed friends," As'hame said, stepping into the dim light of the doorway. "You may call me As'hame, and this is Ti'raon and Ro'molr." He paused with a slight smile. "Mkai told us he has explained our mission to you."

"Mkai?" She glanced at him and he nodded. "These are who you were telling me about?" She turned back to As'hame. "You are the angels?" The last was laced with skepticism.

"Yes, these are whom I told you about." Mkai said, "I told them about you, and what you are doing for me, us, and they wanted to meet with you."

She looked at him and then studied the three angels a moment. "Really?"

"Hah, As'hame, I don't think she believes us," Ro'molr laughed.

"Well, no wonder Ro', you do not really look the part," Ti'raon said, cutting him off.

Ro'molr rubbed his beard and then shrugged.

As'hame shook his head and turned to Rie. Mkai saw the confusion all over her face while she watched the banter between the two. At that moment, he would have doubted, too.

"I am sorry. I know this must come as a shock to you. We do not really match the description given us," As'hame said.

"I think you need to show her." Mkai said, stepping up close to Rie. "Don't be afraid."

"You are right. It will be the quickest way."

"Wait!" Rie cried out, sudden fear lacing through her voice, "I don't need to know to help! You don't have to show me!"

"I know, little one," As'hame said, gently reaching out a hand and cupping her chin. "Knowing was not necessary to gather information. But it is required for what we must ask of you next."

The fear in her eyes cut at Mkai as her eyes darted about frantically, her panic apparent, "But I don't want to know . . ."

"You fear the knowledge, fear the change in your view of the world," As'hame said. "I would not ask this of you lightly. Please trust us in this. You need to know."

"I know, better than anyone, what this means, Rie." Mkai said quietly.

He tried to let all the compassion and love he had show in his eyes when she looked at him. Her foundations of belief were about to be uprooted completely and he wasn't one hundred percent sure she would be able to handle it. He couldn't tell if the knowledge would make Rie's past harder or easier for her to deal with. All he could do is be there for her as much as he could. Mkai didn't want to think about what the future might hold, especially if Paul really was the Son of God.

"Trust me in this; it really is necessary," he said. "Please."

She met his gaze evenly but he saw the fear in her eyes. As'hame stood quietly, Ro'molr and Ti'raon silent, their banter forgotten. Rie looked long and hard at As'hame and the two angels flanking him before turning back to Mkai.

"I trust you, Kai, with my life. If you tell me this is necessary, I will do it."

Mkai felt so much pride and love for her, his voice thickened. "I will not let anyone hurt you, angel or demon," Mkai said, taking both her hands. "I wouldn't have suggested this if I didn't think it was necessary."

She met his eyes for a moment before nodding and turning back to As'hame, "Okay. I'm ready. Show me."

Mkai put his arm around her shoulders and nodded, "Go ahead."

As'hame nodded back and slowly let the restraints on his inner glow fade. They all watched as the hard-edged resolve on Rie's face disappeared and was replaced by deep joy as As'hame slowly lit the alley. At first blending into the light from the door then growing until it lit the section of the alley in which they stood, his glow rose, shining through the sky and bathing the few clouds floating above them.

She couldn't contain her smile or the gasp of joy as both Ro'molr and Ti'raon stepped up beside their leader and dropped their restraints. She closed her eyes in rapture and stood bathed in light, Mkai standing tall beside her, one arm around her.

"It . . . it is beautiful," she whispered. "I can feel them, they're warm. I have never felt so, so at peace and so loved."

"It is but an echo of the peace and love of Heaven, child," Ti'raon answered, so quiet her voice was like a whisper of an echo.

Mkai swallowed hard, struggling to keep the bone-deep sorrow and jealousy of Rie's experience from his face. He met As'hame's even gaze, the understanding and sympathy in it almost overwhelming him. With an effort, he forced himself to look at Rie as she stood quietly, the rapture and joy on her face one of the most beautiful things he had seen since his fall from Heaven. He fought the tears filling his eyes. *It has been so long since I've heard the song of Heaven.* Silence filled the alley as they waited until she slowly opened her eyes with a sigh.

"Thank you. And I do believe now," she said, shivering. "I will never forget that feeling."

The angels seemed pleased at her response. Mkai felt as if a huge weight had been lifted from his heart, one he didn't realize was there. The smile and rapture on her face made it worth it.

"There is more, little one. So much more than just helping you believe." As'hame said, "We need your aid."

"Of course! I already said I would help you in your search."

"The search may already be over."

She glanced at Mkai in surprise, "But if you've found Him what do you need from me?"

"I don't quite know how to say this but," Mkai said gently, taking a deep breath, "we think your new friend, Paul, may be the one we're searching for."

"What? Paul?" she said, stepping back, her eyes wide.

"There is definitely something special about him. I sensed it when we met at the bar. His touch. Shaking his hand. There is no doubt in my mind."

"But I need to meet him, and then we will know for sure," As'hame said. "I will be able to sense whether it is his connection to Heaven or something else."

Rie put out an arm for support, visibly shaken. Mkai put his arm around her and felt her trembling. His heart threatened to break in his chest from the pain in her voice.

"You're right, there is something special about him; I knew it the moment we met. That's why . . ." she trailed off, head drooping down.

Ti'raon stepped up and gently cupped Rie's chin, slowly raising it.

"That is why you have fallen in love with him. And now you fear you have lost him before you had a true chance. That he is out of reach," she whispered.

Rie slowly nodded as a tear rolled down her cheek.

"Do not despair. I was there when He walked the first time. He loved and was loved in return. As He was then, He is still a man, just a very special one." Ti'raon paused. Resolution and determination filled her face. "We will just have to make sure this time it ends differently."

Mkai watched as Rie nodded again, a small, tremulous smile struggling for life. He wished he had comfort to offer, but Ti'raon knew better what his friend needed.

"It will be okay, little one," Ti'raon said, enveloping Rie in her arms.

As'hame signaled with a nod of his head and walked with Mkai and Ro'molr a way down the alley, leaving the two in peace for the moment.

"We need to find Paul as soon as we can. Happenstance brought him to us and it can as easily work against us," As'hame said, urgency in his tone.

"We can give her a little time to get used to this can't we?" Mkai asked, concern for Rie overriding any other thoughts.

"Of course, but it must be tonight. And soon. Please do not misunderstand my meaning. One of the last things I want to do is cause her any additional grief. I will spare her as much as I possibly can. What lies before us all will be difficult, as it is." The angel paused and looked at Mkai. "But you also need to understand I can let nothing interfere with finding and keeping Paul safe. If he is, indeed, who we seek."

There was no mistaking the note of command and strength in the last and both Ro'molr and As'hame stared at Mkai until he reluctantly nodded his head. He fully understood the point As'hame made, but he was bound and determined to keep Rie safe, as safe as he could, both physically and emotionally. Mkai stared back at As'hame in silence, letting the angel see the certainty in his eyes. His defiance weakened at the compassion and understanding in As'hame's face and he couldn't help but fidget as they waited.

The silence finally got to Mkai and he opened his mouth to say something, anything, when Ti'raon motioned them over. Mkai went straight to his friend and assumed his position beside her, one hand on her shoulder. She looked at him with gratitude before turning to face As'hame.

"I'm sorry for breaking down. I understand how important this is," Rie said.

"We understand. There is nothing for which to apologize." The angel's smile was kind and gentle.

"You need to meet him, when? How soon?"

"As soon as possible. Tonight if we can," As'hame said. "It is vital we determine whether he is who we think he is and protect him."

"I don't know where he lives but I can call him."

"Please do."

Rie took a deep breath, "Okay, my phone's in my purse under the bar."

Mkai led her into the building, leaving As'hame to take one last look around the alley. He noticed the angel seemed uneasy, as if something felt amiss. At Mkai's questioning glance, As'hame merely shrugged as he and Ti'raon and Ro'molr followed Mkai into the bar.

None saw a shadow break free and move from behind the dumpster. A silhouette broke the skyline and the two figures looked at each other before moving away from the bar.

CHAPTER NINETEEN

Rie closed her phone with a snap as she turned to As'hame.

"Ok, I asked him if I could come over. Told him there was something I needed to talk to him about."

"And he didn't question that?" Mkai asked.

"I could tell it made him curious, but he seemed willing to wait. I didn't tell him about any of you."

"Good, we need to get going," Ti'raon said urgently.

"He said it would take about ten minutes to drive to his place from here," she said, outlining Paul's address on a napkin.

"One can travel faster than five."

"I can't just leave. I'm the only one here." Rie protested.

"Is there someone you can call?" Mkai said.

"Let me call Rick, he's the other night bartender." She waited long enough for As'hame to nod and flipped open her cell again.

"Hey Rick, it's Rie. Are you busy?"

"Rie! How's it goin' girl!" Rick's enthusiastic greeting made her smile as it always did. "I'm not doing much, just watching TV. What's up?"

"Can you come cover my shift? Something's come up and I really gotta jet."

"Sure thing, I can be there in fifteen minutes."

"Ah thanks Rick, I owe you one," Rie said, giving As'hame a thumbs up. "See you then." She stowed her phone back in her purse and said, "He'll be here in fifteen or so and then I'm free to go."

"Thank you, Rie. Ordinarily, I would hesitate splitting our group," As'hame said, "but in this case, Ti'raon, I think we might be wise to take some precautions."

"I am on my way," Ti'raon said, anticipation bringing her off the barstool to her feet.

"Do not interact with him, yet. Just watch, make sure he is safe and there is no threat. It will take us between twenty and thirty minutes to get there," As'hame cautioned.

"Yes, M'hablis," she said with a quick nod.

As'hame watched as she slipped through the back door, appearing surprised and touched.

"What are your thoughts?" Ro'molr paused, "M'hablis," he continued with a small grin.

Rie looked back and forth between the two companions as they gazed at each other in silence, the bar music an odd background for the formality on their faces.

"M'hablis?" Rie asked.

"I am sorry, it is a title of sorts among us, and not one I expected to hear," As'hame said.

"The closest your language comes to is 'general' but there's so much more to it." Ro'molr said. "A M'hablis is the epitome of what we stand for—they are the bulwark against evil, the standard to which we hold ourselves. Their word is law but there is nothing any would not do if asked." He paused, his joking manner gone completely, and Rie saw for the first time the As'rai Ro'molr as he stood tall, gaze focused on his leader. "We would follow him to the Gates of Hell and beyond. Our lives before his."

His quiet resolve touched Rie as Ro'molr bowed his head before the tall angel. "M'hablis."

She watched in silence as As'hame reached out a hand to grip his friend's shoulder. "My friend."

The two stood a moment and embraced as soldiers, as brothers.

They broke apart and As'hame took a deep breath. "An honor and responsibility unexpected but I will do my best to be worthy."

He glanced at Rie who stood with Mkai. "My thought is this. We need to get to Paul as soon as possible. Ti'raon should be there by now and she will watch over him. But we need to be ready to take him to a safe place as soon as we arrive."

"Since we have time, can I have a beer?" Ro'molr grinned.

At As'hame's nod, Rie slipped behind the bar.

"It is lucky for you alcohol does not affect us," As'hame said, a silver thread of laughter in his voice making both Mkai and Rie smile.

"Lucky me," Ro'molr said as Rie set the beer in front of him.

"Do they really exist?" Rie said, checking her watch as Ro'molr drained half his glass in one gulp.

"Do what exist?" As'hame asked, leaning against the bar.

"Gates to Hell?"

"I do not know, child. Hell, and the final fall, happened after my brethren and I left Heaven and came to Earth. We know of the events and the aftermath and some few other details that have been shared. But we know nothing of Gates."

"I do," Mkai answered quietly. "There are six main Gates scattered around the world."

"Main Gates?" As'hame asked, interrupting.

"Yes, six main Gates, and several small ones that few know about."

"Interesting. We may need to speak further upon that." Rie felt As'hame had a few ideas and wasn't sure if Mkai was going to like them.

"Rick should be here in a couple minutes. What's our next step?" Rie asked, taking the empty glass from Ro'molr.

"We take Paul to a safe location. Ti'raon should be close by, protecting him, but the sooner we get there, the better I will feel." As'hame motioned everyone close.

"Normally, we would fly but we do not have that option so driving will be the best bet."

"I do have a car; it's just up the street," Rie said, "But . . ." She trailed off, a flush spreading across her cheeks, "It's only a little two-seater VW Bug."

"And we will not all fit." As'hame finished her thought. "It will still work. I will go with you, Rie." To Ro'molr he said, "That means you take Mkai and fly above us."

Mkai groaned as Ro'molr grinned and clapped him on the shoulder.

"Understood, M'hablis. I will be close by if I am needed."

"Try not to get too far ahead in case we have trouble. We will have to follow the streets so our travel will be slower."

Mkai gingerly rubbed his shoulder where the exuberant angel had clapped him. If that was a friendly blow, Rie definitely did not envy Mkai.

The door to the bar opened and Rie motioned to Rick before turning to As'hame and the others.

"Rick is here. Give me a chance to talk to him and we can go. Go on to the back room."

Rie watched Mkai and the two angels move through to the back.

"Thanks, Rick, I really appreciate this."

"No problem, Rie, is there anything I can do?" he said, slipping out of his jacket.

"No, but thank you."

"Ok. I got this; get on outta here."

Once again, Rie felt grateful for her friends and their acceptance. She knew he was probably quite curious about Mkai and the others when they slipped through the back, but he wouldn't ask any questions. She smiled then gathered her jacket and purse. She shook her head as she walked through the back. Things were going so fast; there was so much at stake.

Mkai and his two companions were waiting as Rie stepped into the alley.

"I'm ready."

"Very well, Ro'molr," As'hame nodded.

Rie could see Mkai tense as Ro'molr stepped up behind him.

"No pretending to drop me this time," he said as Ro'molr wrapped his arm around his chest.

"You can trust me. Try to relax. The more relaxed you are, the easier it will be," Ro'molr said. "At least for me."

Mkai had a moment to grin at Rie before, with a hard leap, Ro'molr pulled him into the air. His wings thrust hard sending them up into the night.

A laugh trailed behind them as they disappeared and Rie realized that Mkai sounded like he was totally enjoying this adventure. Nervous, she turned to where As'hame stood patiently waiting. Without Mkai, Rie felt adrift and at the mercy of the events unfolding around her.

"Be easy, little one," As'hame said quietly. "Nothing has changed. Your friend is still here with us, just up there, instead."

Faint laughter reached her ears from where Mkai soared, unseen in the darkness. She nodded to As'hame and led the way to her car.

She slid in behind the steering wheel and, leaning over, unlocked the passenger door. As'hame eased his tall length in, knees tight against the dash. He reached under the seat and slid it all the way back

"That is better," he said pulling his seat belt across his lap.

"Yeah, they're not really made for angels I guess," Rie said.

"Not really, but then few things are."

She opened her mouth to ask a question but then thought better of it. Her hope it had gone unnoticed was in vain.

"Please do not fear me. You may ask me any questions you have. I will tell you what I can."

"It's a stupid question."

"Knowledge is gained by questions so, please, continue."

"Well, I just wondered, when you said things aren't made for angels. I'm sure it's not that comfortable for you and you had mentioned flying isn't allowed. I wondered why."

"Ah, it is one of the restraints put upon us by God. He commanded us to bow down before Man. That was actually a catalyst for the war, but one of the tenants of it is that we are not permitted to lift a son of earth and water from the ground. Thus, flying with a human is not allowed."

"Is hiding your true appearance also a rule?" she asked, slowing for a four-way stop, sliding through after checking for other traffic.

"That is more of a choice of my order, that and cloaking ourselves from human view. Unlike demons, who can only disguise themselves from you with a glamour, we have the ability to hide ourselves completely, to become invisible. Thus, we rarely have to reveal ourselves to humans."

"You don't show yourselves normally? What exactly does your order do?"

His chuckle made her think she had said something stupid but was relieved when he smiled at her. "We watch over you. We keep the demons away when we can."

"I can't imagine the things you've seen, the knowledge of our history you must have." She didn't try to disguise the awe in her voice at the thought.

"I have seen a lot. Combined, our order has probably memory of virtually every step of your evolution."

"Is it written down anywhere?" she asked, feeling her curiosity come alight.

"No, we have never had the need. We are all blessed with a perfect memory," he said with a shrug.

"Oh, that's too bad." she couldn't help the disappointment in her voice.

"When this is all over, perhaps we can set aside a moment if there are particular events you are curious about."

"That would be fantastic! Thank you."

"But, unless I am mistaken, the conversation will have to happen another time as that is our destination up ahead."

"Yes, it is." She shared a look with As'hame as she pulled up to the curb. The dark street seemed full of shadows and she inched forward until they were hidden by a tall eucalyptus, its fragrant scent bringing back childhood memories, not all of them good ones. She turned off the ignition and, taking a deep breath, stepped out onto the deserted street.

"Now what?" she asked, meeting As'hame's calm gaze across the top of her VW.

"Ro'molr should be here with Mkai any moment. Then we find Ti'raon and Paul."

"That was amazing!" Mkai's excited voice interrupted the angel as Ro'molr and his passenger landed with a thump.

Ro'molr rolled his eyes as Mkai hurried over to Rie. "What a ride."

She couldn't help but grin at her friend's excitement. "Ours wasn't quite as interesting."

"I'm not sure interesting is the word I'd use," Ro'molr said. "He was squirming around so much I nearly dropped him several times, in spite of my guarantee."

"That was the first time I could actually enjoy it," Mkai said. "I've always been jealous of those of who could fly, so thank you."

"Are you done?" Ti'raon's cautious whisper came out of the darkness. "You're making noise enough for everyone to hear."

They all turned to her as she slipped from the darkness. "He is safe. I did a sweep two blocks out and I didn't sense anything."

"Excellent. Thank you Ti'raon," As'hame said with a nod.

"What's next?" Rie asked.

"The next part hinges on you, Rie. You have to get us in to see him," As'hame said. "We need time to convince him without being thrown out."

"I will do my best."

"This way," Ti'raon said, leading them across the street.

"He said that he lives on the top floor," Rie said. "How should I do this?"

"Go up alone to talk to him. Explain to him that you have some people he needs to meet." She took some confidence in As'hame's belief in her.

"When you do, close the drapes on his balcony," As'hame said pointing, "we'll take that as a signal."

"We arrive by air?" Mkai asked "Are you sure?"

"Yes. We need him to believe, and we do not have a lot of time. It's imperative we get Paul to a safe location without attracting any attention. We need to make the biggest impact we can when we meet him."

"Okay," Rie nodded. "Wish me luck."

"Do you think this will work?" she heard Ro'molr murmur as she walked up the steps. She didn't hear the answer as she buzzed the door.

CHAPTER TWENTY

"Come on up," Paul said and hit the buzzer.

He pushed the listen button in time to hear the click of the door closing, butterflies fluttering in his stomach. He quickly checked his apartment. *At least it's clean.*

It wasn't a large apartment. A couch and a small chair facing a flat screen TV on a small stand. A DVD player poked out from underneath. There was just room past the TV to walk out on the balcony where the drapes swung gently in the breeze. He glanced into the small kitchen off to the side, glad he'd done the dishes earlier. With no time to make the bed, he quickly walked down the short hallway and shut the door.

He stepped into the bathroom and ran some water in the sink, getting rid of a trace of toothpaste. He quickly sprayed on a little cologne. He remembered the way the saleswoman reacted when he tested it out. The sigh, almost moan, of pleasure when she held his wrist and sniffed. *How could I not buy it after that?* Paul heard a knock on the door and, glancing in the mirror, tweaked his hair a bit before heading to open it.

"Hi, Paul," Rie said. His heart thumped just seeing her and hearing her voice.

"Come on in," he said, waving her in.

He thought Rie seemed nervous as she walked past him, but he noticed she raised her head, sniffing slightly as she walked by him. He grinned as he closed and locked the door.

"Can I get you something to drink?" he asked as Rie walked toward the pair of bookcases on the wall.

"Some water would be great, thank you," she said, glancing at his framed print of *The Accolade* by Edmund Blair-Leighton. "That's a great print; it's one of my favorites."

"Water it is, and thank you. It's one of my favorites, too."

She smiled at him as he walked into the kitchen.

"I thought you had to work tonight?" he called, grabbing a glass and a pitcher from the fridge.

"I was supposed to but something came up and I had to see you."

"Oh?"

"An interesting collection, I don't recognize many of the authors," she said, ignoring his question. Paul couldn't quite figure out what was so different about her tonight, but he had a feeling something was on her mind. Rie seemed nervous, or apprehensive. He wasn't one to pry. She'd tell him when she was ready, he figured.

"I mostly read fantasy fiction, but there are some suspense novels on the bottom there," he said, pointing.

"Those are the only ones I recognize," she said glancing at him. "What are those?"

He looked where she was pointing, "Ah, those. I've collected antique books for years, mostly buying online. The half-dozen there range from one hundred to four hundred years old." He smiled at the look of surprise on her face. "I have some arrowheads that are two thousand years old and coins almost as old. I like old things."

"Wow. I wouldn't have expected that."

He walked over and handed her the glass of cold water. "So. As pleased as I am to see you, I can't help but be curious as to why."

Concern tickled the back of his neck when she avoided his eyes.

"What is it Rie?"

"Please, Paul, can you sit?"

Feeling puzzled and a bit confused, he still thrilled at the way she said his name. He shrugged and moved over to the chair. He sat as she began to pace, sipping her water and still avoiding his gaze.

"What is it?" he asked again, not even trying to disguise the concern in his voice.

"Do you trust me?" she blurted.

Paul didn't hesitate. "Yes."

His simple statement stopped her pacing and she stood and looked at him. The certainty in his voice surprised him, too, but he realized that he did. He did trust her. He wasn't sure why, he hadn't even known her a week. *My instincts are usually good, and there is something about her. After all, she did save my life.*

"I trust you as well, Paul, and that's why I'm here. I want you to meet some people. Some friends of Kai's."

"Is that what has you so nervous you can't sit still?" he said. "Of course I'll meet them, I'd be happy to meet anyone you ask me to."

"Thank you," she smiled with relief. "Please, keep an open mind. They're not . . . well you'll see."

"All right. I promise to keep an open mind," Paul said, leaning back into the couch. Warning bells started in his head at her pause. *What's this all about?*

Keeping her eyes on his, Rie slowly walked backward to the balcony, focused on him. *Something is going to change.* He felt the universe still around the two of them as she slid the balcony door open. *Something big.*

He watched her nod into the darkness and then close the drapes. She began pacing again pulling his attention from the balcony door.

"You asked me to meet some friends of yours but you seem more nervous now than when you asked. Were the drapes a signal? Are they outside? Should I buzz them in?"

"No, Paul, you won't need to let them in," she said as an audible thump came from the balcony, "In fact, they're already here."

"What?" Paul stood. "How?"

"Right here." Mkai stepped into the room from the balcony. "Hello again, Paul."

"Kai?" Paul asked as he recognized him, "but we've already . . ."

"It is not him that she was speaking of."

Paul watched as two men and a woman entered behind Kai. He was struck by the beauty of all three of them. Both men towered over Kai at well over six feet tall. They made the woman seem petite in comparison. He noticed a curious gracefulness to their movement, unusual but almost familiar. Even standing still, he felt an extraordinary quality about them he couldn't define. Something inside Paul resonated, leaving him feeling apprehensive yet excited at the same time.

"I told Rie I would meet her friends, but first someone needs to tell me why she is so nervous about it," Paul said. "And I would like to know how you got on my balcony."

"In good time. You shall have answers to all your questions." said the first man, holding up his hands. "Names first, if you will."

"You know Mkai, or Kai as you call him. This is Ti'raon and Ro'molr. And I am As'hame. It is our distinct pleasure to meet you."

Paul watched in silence as each one mentioned bowed in turn with their hand to their chest in a curious salute.

"Hello," Paul said after a moment. "Now please tell me why you're in my apartment and why Rie is so freaked out."

"I'm not freaked out!" she protested stopping her pacing and stepping up beside him. "It's just really important."

"All right." He could still feel her thrumming with tension. "I've met them, now what?" Paul said, putting his arm around her.

She fell silent and slipped her arm around his waist. Paul relished how natural she felt against him, the heat of her body radiating through his shirt.

As'hame studied him for several minutes in silence, long enough for Paul to start feeling nervous himself. *What is all of this about?* The butterflies in his stomach began fluttering overtime when As'hame and Kai—Mkai, Paul reminded himself—exchanged a knowing look.

"You were right. This close, I can feel it."

"I feel Him as well," Ti'raon said, excitement evident in her voice.

"There is no mistaking Him," Ro'molr said.

Paul felt the tension in the room rise even higher.

"Feel who? What are you talking about?" he said, voice cracking from nerves.

"We don't have a lot of time to cover everything but we will explain what we can," As'hame said motioning them to sit, "And after that, decisions need to be made."

Paul turned to Rie, "Marie, is this what you want? You trust these people?"

"Yes, Paul, it's what I want. I do trust them, with my life," she said, eyes wide.

"That's good enough for me," he said simply and, sitting, pulled her down beside him.

She settled comfortably against him and he pulled her close. He smiled at her soft contented sigh and the way she felt when her head settled on his shoulder. He focused as As'hame stepped up, Mkai, Ti'raon, and Ro'molr taking up positions beside him.

"Paul, Rie told you a little about me." Mkai began first, surprising Paul who expected As'hame to continue, "She's collected information for me for many years now. But she only recently found out why. I've been gathering information for a long, long time. To help me understand."

"Understand what?"

"Mankind. To help me understand the way you think, the way you feel, the way you love."

"Wait, you say that like . . ."

159

"Yes, Paul, I say that like I am not human. That is because we are not," Mkai said simply.

"Ha!"

Paul's laugh obviously caught them all off guard, but this had to be a joke. "Nice, Rie, I didn't know you were into practical jokes. You had me going!" Even as he chuckled, the earnest looks on the faces of the others told him maybe this wasn't much of a laughing matter. Still, he couldn't imagine they were serious.

"You totally got me. I thought there was something serious happening. That you were in trouble."

"Wait, Paul . . ." Rie tried to interrupt.

"Nice! Who are these guys? Some people from work? How did they get on the balcony?" He rose, walking over to open the balcony drapes. "A ladder? Rope?"

"We flew." As'hame's quiet words stopped Paul for a moment. He slowly turned from the outside doors, caught by the tone in the man's voice. It had to be a joke. But something deep inside him told him otherwise.

"Yeah, right. Where's your wings?"

"Right here," Ro'molr said.

Paul started with shock, almost falling against the balcony as Ro'molr lit up with a glow bright enough to light the entire room. More than that, Paul felt a pull, almost a recognition or tie with the light.

Ro'molr stood before Paul suddenly appearing clothed in armor, sword by his side. Paul felt his eyes go wide as Ro'molr slowly stretched out his wings. He stepped back as Ti'raon and As'hame followed suit.

"This is not how I thought to show you, but it will do," As'hame said, holding his arms to the side and bowing his head.

"Wait . . . What . . . Are you . . ." Paul stuttered. "Rie."

"Yes, Paul, they are . . ." she started.

"Angels?" Paul breathed, interrupting her.

"Yes, Paul, we are angels. Here on earth to keep Man safe," As'hame said.

"Well, *they* are."

Paul recognized the sound of longing and bone-deep sorrow filling Mkai's voice.

"They? If you're not an angel . . ." Paul asked motioning between them.

"I am a demon," Mkai said looking carefully at Rie. "I'm sorry, Rie. This is my true appearance, hidden behind illusion all these years."

Paul watched in silence as Mkai almost rippled, his features melting away. Scales started shining softly in the light, cat-slit eyes glowing green.

"I am a demon, cursed with this semblance for my part in the war," he raised his hands, the dull black of his claw-like fingernails stark against his pale hair. He tapped the two small horns sprouting from his temples, "with all that you'd expect. I can hide my appearance when walking among you, but this is my true form."

Rie rose from the couch and approached him, a small frown on her face. She stopped an arm's length away and stared intently into Mkai's sad eyes. Even from where he stood, Paul could see long years of loneliness in the demon's gaze. Rie reached out a hand and softly cupped Mkai's cheek. Paul heard Mkai catch his breath at her touch.

"Demon, you may be, but I still see my friend, Kai," she said softly and then smiled.

His answering smile was unsteady. Paul saw tears slip down Mkai's cheeks as she hugged him to her.

"We see our friend as well," Ti'raon's clear voice fell into the silence as Rie held her friend.

161

CHAPTER TWENTY-ONE

"I don't understand," Paul said. Frustration was making him fidget. It felt like full understanding was dancing at the tip of his consciousness, but could this really be happening? Angels? Demons? *What on earth do they want with me?*

"It's simple really," Mkai said, straightening up as Rie stepped away with a smile. "I switched sides. I learned something, which was the final influence I needed to finally make a decision."

"Decisions, switching sides, are you allowed to do that?"

"Not easily no, but this was too important to not try," Mkai said.

"Please, Paul, be at ease and sit; we will explain it all," said As'hame.

"Be at ease. Yeah, right. Because it's every day I have angels and demons come to my house." Paul didn't even know where to start understanding this madness. *Is this a dream?*

"Come sit, please. It's okay." Rie said, taking his hand and leading him back to the couch.

She sat down, still holding his hand. She met his gaze as Paul studied her. Rie seemed unfazed by this whole thing, and didn't he know from the beginning there was something unusual about her?

The feeling of trust he'd had for her was still the same. Finally, with a nod he turned to the others.

He took a deep breath. "All right. I'm listening, but someone needs to start making sense," he said, settling on the couch, Rie slipping easily under his arm.

"Mkai discovered something he was not supposed to know and came to me," As'hame said, taking over the story. "We have had dealings in the past, he and I. Enough so I gave him a moment to speak before destroying him."

"Destroy?"

"Yes, destroy. Normally angels will destroy my kind when they find them," Mkai said. "My kind is only on earth to sow discord and strife and to corrupt Man."

"You risked a lot to go to him, then."

"His very existence. It is part of the reason I gave him space to explain," As'hame agreed. "That, and because Mkai has never behaved as other demons."

"What did he find out? Now I'm curious," Paul said. He had a feeling he might not like the answers he was about to receive, but listened intently all the same.

"Some background first," As'hame continued. "There really was a war in Heaven. The schism between angels was deep and painful, led by an archangel called Samael. He failed and was thrown from Heaven as punishment for his sins."

"And all who fought with him," Ro'molr added.

"Or who refused to fight against him," Ti'raon said.

"Or just gave away information they shouldn't have," Mkai finished softly.

"As is said, God is a loving God, but He is also a vengeful one," As'hame went on with the story. "Betrayal, He does not accept and is beyond harsh in dealing with it. Those He threw from His Grace suffered for it, in appearance and in being barred from His Light for all eternity."

Mkai stared at the floor, nodding. "And punishment it has been."

"Say I believe all this." Paul still felt puzzled and a bit overwhelmed. But he had never been the type to back down and he didn't feel as if he was getting solid answers. Rie squeezed his hand and he took comfort in the contact. "But what does an ancient war have to do with us now? With me?" he asked.

"Because it appears the war may be starting again."

"Samael wants to go to war again . . . why?" Paul asked, honestly confused. "He didn't learn a lesson the first time?"

"That's the first thing I discovered. It isn't Samael." Mkai answered, "He was overthrown."

"And the new Lord of Hell intends to corrupt Man and convert him to build an army." As'hame's voice sounded disgusted and angry.

Paul shivered. He thought a moment. "And wage war on Heaven using the souls of Man?" It wasn't a question; somehow he knew. *But how did he know?*

"Yes," As'hame said.

"Well, someone needs to stop him."

"Her. The new Lord is female," Mkai interrupted.

"Her. Someone needs to stop her," Paul corrected. "Is that why you're here?"

"Patience. There was a second piece of information Mkai brought to me," As'hame said, "And it is that which has brought my brother and sister here with me, and why my order is sending reinforcements."

"Something bigger than that?" Paul asked, puzzled and totally not liking the turn this conversation was taking. "What could possible matter more?"

"Because God does have a Son," As'hame said softly, "and He has been sent once again to offer salvation to Man." The angel started pacing up and down in front of the couch. Ro'molr took up position by the balcony while Ti'aron slipped over to the door and stood with her arms crossed. *Almost like they're guarding the room. Why? And from what?*

"And that's the information you asked Rie to help with, right?" Paul said. "Finding this guy?"

"Yes." Mkai nodded.

"Where do I come in, how can I help?"

"A few questions first, if I may," As'hame said, stopping his pacing and staring intently at Paul.

"Um. Sure," Paul said, not quite sure where this was going. Rie remained curiously silent, her hand warm in his, and he wondered what she knew, and how long she'd known it. *And how can she handle this so calmly?* Every one of his nerves jangled.

"Your parents, who were they?"

"I never knew. I was left at an orphanage when I was a couple months old. The records were all lost in a fire so I couldn't find out if I wanted to."

"Who raised you?"

"My adoptive parents. They passed away when I was nineteen. They were wonderful and I still miss them."

Paul felt Rie squeeze his hand and he turned and smiled briefly at her and he hugged her a little closer.

"Did you have a pendant, a charm, or a bracelet when you were left at the orphanage?" Ti'raon asked, speaking for the first time.

"Yes," Paul said, surprised. "How did you know? I still do. It's a silver pendant, I've always worn it." He resisted the urge to touch it beneath his shirt.

The angels shared a significant look.

"What do these questions have to do with finding Him? Do you think I might know Him?"

"Something like that," As'hame said.

"Shouldn't he be easy to find, just look for miracles, water into wine kinda thing?"

"It's not that easy," Mkai said.

"He does not know who He is," Ti'raon finished, a curious tone in her voice.

"Well, that does make it harder, doesn't it?" Paul couldn't imagine what they were getting at.

"Perhaps," As'hame spoke, "It also keeps Him safe."

"I suppose. How can I help you find Him?" Paul was more than willing to help these people. He wasn't sure he bought the whole story; Angels and demons? A war? It was a little much to take in all at once but the proof something strange was happening was hard to overlook.

"We think we might have found Him already," As'hame said.

"Really? Who is He? Someone famous, I bet!" Paul said, leaning forward with excitement, "It is L.A. after all."

"He's not famous yet," Rie said, placing her hand on his shoulder.

Paul looked at her then back to As'hame. He stopped at the steady gaze meeting his eyes. The same expression was mirrored in Ti'raon, as well as Ro'molr and again echoed in Mkai's eyes.

Paul started to feel a little nauseous. No. It couldn't be. No way. He looked to Rie. "Wait . . ."

"Yes, Paul," she began gently, "we believe it's you."

"What!" He jumped to his feet, heart thumping in his chest. "No way! I'm just a regular guy! I'm nobody!"

"You are far more than that," she interrupted taking his hand, "even if you aren't who we're searching for."

He opened his mouth to reply but couldn't think of a word to say. Rie held him with her eyes and he felt the beginnings of panic slow. "But I'm not anyone important. I work at UPS." he argued.

"Do you think the world knew who He was the first time?" Ti'raon said. "I was there, before anyone else. I knew Him and saw Him and no one else knew who He was or what He was there to do until the time came."

Paul met her steady gaze and felt some of his fear fade.

"But how do you know? How can you be sure?"

167

"We can feel the touch of God. Standing here, in this room with you, the air hums with it," As'hame said. "There is no mistaking it. I am certain of it. You are who we seek."

Paul squeezed his eyes shut, panic starting to flood his senses again. "But I'm not special. I sink swimming in the ocean like anyone else." He opened his eyes. "I don't even like wine and sure can't turn water into it! I don't even go to church."

As'hame snorted. "As if going to church has anything to do with this. Your powers are dormant. No one knows how or when they will manifest. But I do know, sooner or later, they will begin to show," As'hame said. "From what I can sense from you, I think they have already started to show in little ways."

"Wait," Ro'molr interrupted holding up his hand, head cocked to the side.

As one, the angels turned to the balcony, heads swiveling back and forth.

"We are out of time," As'hame said.

"What is it?" Mkai walked over and stood with the three angels.

"There are more than a dozen demons approaching," Ti'raon said.

"Demons? Like Mkai?"

"No. Not like Mkai," As'hame said.

Paul watched him shift his stance, like he was readying himself for a fight. *Well, this can't be good*, Paul's stomach lurched. *What did As'hame mean, not like Mkai?*

"We must get him out of here," Ti'raon touched As'hame's arm.

"There aren't that many, we could take them," Ro'molr put his hand on his sword hilt.

"We could," As'hame nodded, "and if we were alone, we would do so. But we cannot risk Paul and Rie, nor the attention that it would draw."

"You and Mkai take them to safety. Ti'raon and I can handle this," Ro'molr said.

"But I . . ." Ti'raon didn't look like she wanted any part of this plan, and Paul wondered if what she said earlier about the two of them was actually true.

"The demons cannot catch up to us. They must be stopped, or delayed long enough for us to get free. I must stay with them. I need you and Ro'molr to do this," As'hame said holding her gaze.

"You are right," she sighed. "You must get them to safety, Ro'molr and I will do this. I failed him once. I will not fail him again."

Paul watched this exchange, mesmerized. *Was this really happening?*

"They may have someone watching. We need to leave unseen," As'hame said.

Paul brought himself back to the present with a jerk. "There's a cellar entrance kind of hidden by bushes in the backyard." Right now, if there was danger, Rie was his first priority. He couldn't let anything happen to her.

"That will work. The four of us shall take that route. Ti'raon, Ro'molr, you know what to do. Hit them before they arrive and hold them. We need at least ten minutes to get clear but the more time you give us the better."

"Understood."

"Ro'molr, Ti'raon is in charge. When she says break away, break away. We need you both. I cannot keep them safe for long on my own." Paul did not mistake the stern tone in As'hame's voice. Apparently, neither did Ro'molr, from the disappointed look on his face.

"I understand."

"I will give you as much time as we can before we break free. We will try to lead them away as well." Ti'raon's steely gaze removed any doubt from Paul she meant business. And he guessed he was now Ti'raon's business. He wasn't sure how to feel about that.

"Excellent. Find us in three hours," As'hame said and paused. "Remind them."

Paul watched as the two angels turned to look at their leader.

"Remind them why they should fear us. Show them what this war will bring. Show them why we are God's Soldiers."

As'hame's words sent a thrill through Paul. He had imagined scenes likes this, his favorite books were full of them. He had never imagined he would actually experience it, let alone have it centered on him. *Can they really think I'm the Son of God?*

The two angels nodded and, with a final bow to Paul and Rie, they saluted their leader. Curtains brushed pearly wings as they slipped out to the balcony. Paul watched them leap into the night sky before turning back to As'hame.

"Where are we going?" Paul stood, pulling Rie up beside him. Her hand trembled in his, although, at this point, Paul wasn't sure if it was her trembling or his. This was all happening so fast he could hardly think.

"I do not know yet. Events are evolving quicker than I expected."

"I have an idea" Mkai said. "We need to see him anyway, and I think he will have what we need."

"Ah, Roger?" As'hame smiled. "Excellent. We will go there first. Paul, will you show us this cellar so we can get out of here?"

"Of course," he said. "It's downstairs behind the furnace."

"Wait, how will we travel?" Mkai asked.

Rie finally spoke. "Yeah, we won't all fit in my car."

"We'd fit in mine," Paul suggested.

The angel nodded. "That will work. It would be dangerous to separate us further," As'hame said. "We need to go. Time is short."

Paul nodded then had a thought.

"Just one second," he said and hurried to the bedroom. He slid open the dresser and, reaching in, pulled out the Glock hidden there. He had bought it for protection years ago when the neighborhood started declining. He'd gone through all the safety classes and used it enough to be comfortable. Paul wasn't sure how effective a gun would be against demons but better to be prepared. *Demons? Did I really just think that?*

He clipped the holster on his belt, tucking it into the back of his pants. Checking the magazine and seeing it fully loaded, Paul slipped it into the holster. He pulled his shirt over it as he grabbed a jacket and left the room. He wasn't leaving Rie's safety up to strangers, angels or not.

"Okay, let's go," Paul said. He grabbed his keys and, taking Rie's hand, led her to the door. He took one last look around his simple apartment and wondered if he'd see it again.

CHAPTER TWENTY-TWO

The demons crawled along the rooftop, whispering to each other as they moved through the shadows. The harsh, guttural language of Hell tore at the air, bruising the silence. Ti'raon and Ro'molr hovered above them in silence, waiting for the moment to strike. The two angels watched in barely controlled anger and disgust as the demons slunk and skittered as their natures dictated. There were a lot more than a mere half-dozen. Evidently, something had tipped the creatures as to Paul's identity and location.

Ti'raon shared a look with her partner, joined in their distaste of the creatures before them. They turned back as the demons slowed their crawl and came together in a group, jostling and growling at one another. Ti'raon shot a glance to Ro'molr, voicing her opinion on the chaos below with a simple nod.

Ro'molr grinned and drew his blade. "Remind them," he said. His whisper barely made it to Ti'raon's ear as she slowly drew her blade as well.

They separated and, as one, dove at their enemies below.

The surprise was total as the two angels swept down in silence, their swords sending two demons to their deaths on the first pass. They were able to cross over twice more before the demons realized they were under attack. Half a dozen of the vile creatures were down, blood spilling across the roof. Harsh growls were turning to howls of dismay as the beasts spun trying to see their attackers. The angels swept down again, darting in and out of the darkness, shock and fear taking control of the crowded brutes. Ti'raon drove her blade through a scaled chest as she flew by, blood spraying the air when she pulled it free. The fiends pushed in on themselves as those on the outer ring tried to push away from the death that seemed all around them. Panic began to take hold as the crush of bodies grew.

"HOLD!"

The shout resonating from the shadows startled the two darting angels as much as it did the gathered monsters.

"There are only two of the damned As'rai. Spread out and take them!" A shadow emerged from the gloom, standing head and shoulders above the rest. "We rule the darkness. We give fear; we do not suffer it!"

Misshapen forms came rushing out of the murk, doubling the force gathered.

Ti'raon glanced at Ro'molr as the demons started to spread out on the rooftop. She could see lights starting to come on as the noise of battle echoed down to the streets. *Someone will call the police soon, time is slipping away.* She finally recognized the creature threatening and beating the others into a semblance of order. Szafal. He was not the greatest of opponents but not one to be taken lightly either. *If he's here, this battle is a little more critical.*

"They need more time," Ti'raon said. "And if Szafal is here, there might be less of it than we thought. Especially if the police reach us before we're done."

Ro'molr shrugged, his silhouette barely visible in the night sky. "Then we give it to them. Our blood before theirs."

They shared a final look and turned back to the gathering below them. Outnumbered much greater than before, with the element of surprise lost and the demons separated as they were, Ti'raon realized that this might very well be their final battleground.

"AS'RAI!" the two angels cried as they dove at their enemy. Ti'raon resolved to give her M'hablis the time and space he needed to get clear with Paul.

The ancient battle cry of the angels cowed them enough that the two were able to sweep in and safely out once and then again. Monsters were dropping, their gurgling death cries lost in the cacophony of their brethren. Their luck could not last.

With a wild swing, more from fear than an actual attack, Ti'raon saw a sword strike Ro'molr's wing as he darted in. Not much, barely a touch, but enough to throw him off balance. Enough for him to falter and crash into the ranks below. Instead of fighting for height, he let himself go. Ti'raon watched as he fell with the crash, turning it into a rolling twist. He knocked a number of bodies sprawling before rising to his feet, his back to the edge of the roof.

"Quail in fear, spawn of Hell!" he bellowed defiantly, "I am RO'MOLR. Hear my name and COWER! Come join your brothers and sisters whose lives I've torn out. Know the fear and the pain they felt from the thrust of my blade."

His taunts drew all eyes to him as he stood waiting. Ti'raon recognized what he was doing. Trying to give her a chance to escape. A quick glance was all she needed to realize that he would be overwhelmed quickly. *As'hame needs more time.* The thud of her boots on the rooftop beside him caused the crowding monsters to draw away.

"Not alone, my friend," she said. "Ti'raon is my name. It is known to few for rarely do they survive the meeting." She let her restraints fall and as her inner glow lit the sky, "Come then, come and learn the reason why."

The crush of fiends before them muttered and jostled in fear as Ro'molr, too, let his glow shine forth. The gift of God's love given to every angel made the black evil in front of them cringe in fear.

"There are only two. Forward, you cowards, or Kalia will make you wish you had fallen to these!" cried Szafal, striking at the cringing brutes with the flat of his blade. "Forward!"

Ti'raon set herself, determined to kill as many as possible before she fell. The slow creep of the demons before them turned to a rush as they surged forward. She felt Ro'molr slip apart a little, giving her space to swing her blade and to move without allowing an enemy to come between them. As the first rank came within sword's reach she heard the gurgle of death as Ro'molr's blade darted out and decapitated his first target.

Ours before theirs. Ti'raon slipped her blade between the ribs of one scaled form even as she ducked under the wild swing of another. *I failed once before. I will not fail again.*

She swept her blade across, disemboweling her opponent and letting the thrust of another slide past. Her blade danced, drawing blood and death as she slipped past the blades of her enemies. She heard the crashes and howls of fear as Ro'molr brought them to battle, his prowess beating back all attackers. With her vulnerable side protected Ti'raon let herself go, losing herself in the battle rush.

The two angels fought against overwhelming odds, holding back the crush of fiends facing them, their glow lighting the battlefield like it was day. Ro'molr started to sing, the ancient battle hymn, announcing to all with the power to hear it, that here, As'rai did battle. That here, on this lonely, dark rooftop, the first battle of the coming war was being fought. Ti'raon raised her voice, her clear vibrant tone joining his as demons continued to fall before her.

Ti'raon had a moment to think that perhaps all was not lost. Just a moment. Then she staggered to the side as Ro'molr crashed into her, a gunshot echoing in the air. She barely deflected a blow to her head as she tried to keep from falling. If she lost her footing, both she and Ro' were dead. She risked a look at him and saw blood pouring from a wound to Ro'molr's shoulder.

"Ro'molr!" she cried.

He struggled to remain standing, switching his sword to his other hand. "They're using guns. How mundane," he managed to say with his usual grin.

Even now, he jokes. Ti'raon could not let her concern distract her from her mission.

The guttural cries of the beasts swept over them, full of anger and lust. Ti'raon felt fear for the first time in her existence. Demons were never gentle with the angels they captured. What they did to female angels who fell into their hands, she couldn't bear to think about. The depravity of Man was nothing when compared to the nightmare which would engulf her if she allowed these dark creatures to take her alive.

"Go!" Ro'molr grunted, ducking a wild swing and sinking his sword in a creature's belly before pushing it back. "Over the roof, get out of here."

She had no time to answer as they pushed through her attack and Ti'raon felt their vile touch as first one and then another grabbed at her.

"Ro'molr!" she cried out as a demon jumped from the ledge behind them.

Ro'molr began to turn and was pierced from the side even as it crashed in to him. She watched her friend fall under an avalanche of horned, scaled forms. The creatures crowded her against the waist-high ledge so tightly she couldn't reach him. She gave into despair and, with a final glance toward Ro'molr, tried to tip herself over backwards. If she could get over the edge, maybe they'd let go long enough for her to get airborne. If not . . . Normally, a fall from this height wouldn't be fatal but if she let herself fall headfirst. *Maybe if you're lucky you won't survive it.*

"I don't think so."

Szafal reached through the crush surrounding her and grabbing her shoulder, pulled her back from the edge. "You're not getting away that easy."

She stumbled and almost fell from the weight of demons dragging at her as he leered. *I'm sorry As'hame. I hope we gave you enough time. Maybe they will be so busy with me they will forget about you.* She fought a shudder of disgust as they pawed at her, touching her in places that had never felt another's touch.

"STOP!" Szafal cried out, his deep voice cutting across the clamor.

"You scum get on with your task," he scowled at them in disgust. "You who cowered in fear get no share of the spoils. Keep tracking As'hame and the traitor Mkai and find out what they know before killing them."

The creatures started to separate into two groups, snarls of hate and anger overridden by howls of derision. The scream of the approaching sirens were so close that, for a moment, Ti'raon almost hoped for their interference. *Would the demons stop if humans came onto the roof?*

"AS'RAI!" The cry startled all as a cadre angels came streaking in, just barely clearing the rooftop, before crashing into the creatures surrounding her and Ro'molr.

Ti'raon fell to her knees beside Ro'molr as the monsters scattered. The bone deep despair took all her energy as it drained away, replaced with relief. She had never really felt fear before and its aftermath made her shake as the As'rai formed a wall around them. Their voices lifted in the battle hymn as they pressed forward, demons falling over themselves to escape. They had cowered in fear from two; they ran in terror from the might of the eight before them.

Szafal stood ready as the wall of angels flowed around him. Ti'raon didn't recognize the tall As'rai who stopped before the hideous monster.

She watched as Szafal leapt forward, blade swinging up and across in a blinding arc, to be met briefly and deflected, sparks flying from the impact. He struck again and again, thrusting and slashing. Each were blocked and parried, almost casually. His troops behind him falling, their death cries a background dirge as Ti'raon watched Szafal fight the elegant angel.

Suddenly he screamed, his voice full of anger, and sweeping his blade high, swung down as hard as he could. The As'rai before him slipped to the side, letting the wild swing slide by and, almost gently, buried his blade in Szafal's chest. The demon's eyes shot wide in shock and he opened his mouth trying to speak. Whatever words he meant to say were lost in the rush of blood. With a gurgle, he dropped to his knees, hands grasping weakly at the sword. The As'rai lifted a booted foot and, placing it on Szafal's chest, pushed him over onto his back, twisting the blade as it came free, dripping in gore.

He stood over Szafal as he convulsed, arms falling open as he collapsed. Wiping his blade clean, the As'rai turned to Ti'raon and Ro'molr.

He was dressed the same as all the other angels, even Ti'raon and Ro'molr. Silver armor, boots, greaves, and gauntlets, all glinting in the moonlight as he pulled them off. But, somehow, it seemed more majestic on him. His dark hair swept back over dark eyes, his mouth twisted into a condescending smirk as he approached them. Ti'raon struggled to her feet, pulling Ro'molr up beside her as he approached and bowed.

"I am Co'tul. T'alw sent me and these few on as soon as we answered the summons."

"You have impeccable timing and you're my new best friend," Ro'molr said with a tight grin. "I had almost started to think we couldn't beat them all."

Ti'raon formally bowed to their rescuer, "I am Ti'raon and this is Ro'molr. We thank you for your timely assistance. We would not have lasted much longer."

"I am glad that we pushed on through the night," he said. "We were just approaching the outskirts when my scouts reported your glow. We came as quickly as we could."

"We are most grateful." She regarded the creatures sprawled about, grotesque even in death, her eyes drawn to the small knot of angels in a corner. Co'tul's features went hard as stone as they separated, showing the pristine white cloak of one of their own draped over a body still in death. Ti'raon's heart filled with sadness at the death as one of the As'rai approached, grief etching age onto the normally ageless face.

"Se'tha has fallen," the angel said quietly at his leader's nod. "But she took three with her even as she fell."

"She was one of the bravest of us. I never thought I would see her fall," Co'tul said sadly. "Our mortality is one of the prices we pay for being As'rai, she knew and accepted that. Her sacrifice will not be forgotten."

He paused as another As'rai approached and addressed his leader. "We killed almost all of them, perhaps as many as five escaped. Do you want us to pursue?"

"No," Co'tul said, "those few aren't as important as our mission. Call everyone back. We have one of our own to mourn."

The As'rai nodded, his face tight with anger and grief, clapping a hand to his chest before darting away, a horn lifting to his lips.

"We need to get off this roof; someone called the police and they will be here soon," Ro'molr grunted, pain obvious in his voice.

"We do not run from humans. They will not see us unless we allow it. I assume that we lost Se'tha for a reason beyond simply rescuing two As'rai?" Co'tul said, jaws clenched with anger and grief, a peal of light an odd echo to his tone as the horn rang out.

"Yes. As'hame and the others needed time to get clear," Ti'raon said. She understood his grief. The loss of any As'rai was a loss of a brother or sister. She knew exactly how it felt and didn't take his words personally. *This is too important for pettiness, anyway.*

Ro'molr made no qualms about how he felt being discounted. "Se'tha fell in battle to save us and in doing so, perhaps has saved the world. Not quite as simple as you may think."

"Others?" Co'tul stepped closer. "Do you mean . . ."

"We don't know for certain," Ti'raon interrupted shooting a look of warning at Ro'molr, "but perhaps. We need to get back to them and Ro'molr needs his wound tended."

"This is promising news," Co'tul said. "We need to say goodbye to Se'tha before she fades but I will send out scouts to find the others of your party."

He nodded to them both before turning and walking to where the others stood gathered around their fallen sister, waiting for him.

"That was good timing on his part." Ro'molr said as he carefully sat, armor disappearing at a thought, replaced by his casual clothes.

"Indeed, more than just luck has been following us, I am starting to think." Ti'raon said, eyes glued to the group of As'rai who had saved them.

A glittering stream of light began to stretch toward the heavens as the fallen angel started to fade. The As'rai gathered around her responded, their inner glows lighting the roof like it was noon.

"Goodbye, my sister, your noble sacrifice will not be in vain," Ti'raon whispered, letting her inner glow shine forth.

After a moment, the group broke apart and Co'tul made his way to where Ti'raon stood beside Ro'molr.

"We have said goodbye to our fallen comrade, and I have sent scouts out to find a trace of As'hame and the others. The police have entered the building and are making their way to the roof. They have also sent for a helicopter. They may not be able to see us, but remaining here much longer serves little purpose. We will move to another rooftop as soon as Ri'vol tends to your wounds."

An As'rai approached, unslinging a bag, and knelt beside Ro'molr, motioning him to take off his shirt. His tone reassured Ti'raon and she finally felt herself start to relax. She watched the crisp, careful way the As'rai started to clear the rooftop. The way they worked together, not only in battle but in the aftermath, spoke of a group long familiar with each other.

Co'tul motioned to his unit. "T'alw and the Council have used me and my squad for many missions over the centuries."

"You're one of the La'sfo!" Ro'molr suddenly blurted. "I've never met one."

"Yes, we are one of the La'sfo," Co'tul said with a nod. "The Council has a dozen squads, utilized for critical missions or whenever one or two As'rai are deemed not enough for a job. We were the closest. We were in Las Vegas when I got the message."

Co'tul paused. "As soon as Ri'vol finishes, we will move to that rooftop and once my scouts return, we will continue on. I have been told As'hame watches over this city and he is to retain command."

"Yes, the M'hablis keeps this city and our charge, safe," Ti'raon said as Ri'vol started winding a bandage around Ro'molr's shoulder and chest.

"M'hablis? He declared himself?" Co'tul said quirking an elegantly shaped eyebrow.

"No. He did not. I did." Ti'raon returned his steely gaze.

"And I, too, so named him," Ro'molr added, looking up at Co'tul. "He has been named M'hablis, and has accepted the honor. I have never met one more deserving, or one more worthy."

"He is the M'hablis," Ti'raon finished softly.

"Then I look forward to meeting this paragon," Co'tul said.

Ti'raon could not quite interpret the expression upon his face. She hoped the declaration she and Ro'molr made would not cause problems. Angels were, by definition, created without sin. Yet Samael was an example that even angels could give in to sin and fall. And she knew pride was the most insidious of all sins, easily overlooked and capable of making the greatest of them slip. Watching the way Co'tul directed the As'rai in his squad, she wondered how easily he would give up command.

CHAPTER TWENTY-THREE

The soft banging on the door was going on for a while before it intruded enough to bring Roger out of his reverie where he sat in his worn chair. He slowly rose and moved toward the door, carefully, in the characteristic gait of the elderly who lived alone. He reached a hand out to the wall to steady himself and then peeked through the peephole. *You don't need another black eye.* He grinned in relief when he saw who was on the other side.

"Kai!" he exclaimed, struggling with the locks. "One moment!"

He slipped the door open a bit, the specially shortened security chain allowing a bare finger's width of space. After checking Kai was alone, he smiled at his friend and, closing the door, removed the chain. He swung the door wide and motioned Mkai inside. "Please c-come in."

"Thank you, Roger," Mkai said stepping past his friend. "No sausages today?"

Roger chuckled as he closed the door and engaged all the locks, slipping the chain on last. "No, had p-potatoes."

He gestured at the couch as he eased down on his weathered chair and fidgeted around. "P-please be comfortable." Roger leaned back with a sigh "Ah, at my age it can sometimes t-take a bit to get comfortable."

"Yes, but when you get there, it's worth the struggle."

Roger laughed. "It is."

Mkai said, "Sorry to rush things, but have you had a chance to gather what I asked for?"

"Yes," Roger nodded, not really surprised at Mkai's hurry. "I d-doubled the ammunition."

"Thank you, my friend. It's more important than ever now," Mkai said. "Where is it?"

"H-hidden," Roger said, "in the abandoned lot down the s-street."

"Excellent thinking!"

Roger smiled, pleased at the response, and, reaching into the pocket of his worn sweater, tossed Mkai the keys. "H-here."

"Thank you, I can't tell you how much help you've been."

The soft knock at the door startled Roger and he looked at Kai with concern. *What could be going on?* Roger never asked questions, but he could tell, for the first time, Kai seemed on edge.

Kai hurried to the door with his fingers to his lips. He approached the door as quiet as a whisper. Roger watched him stand close, head cocked to the side for a moment before looking through the peephole. He straightened, relief evident in his posture. He smiled at Roger as he started undoing the locks, "It's okay, they are my friends."

Roger struggled to his feet as the door swung wide to show three people standing in the hallway, two men and one woman. Now, he was really troubled. Until now, very few people knew where he lived, and that was just the way Roger wanted it. *What is Kai thinking?*

"Please, don't worry," Kai said reassuringly. "These are friends; they mean you no harm. You know I would never do anything to put you in danger."

Roger didn't know what to think. He trusted Kai, but few, very few, people knew where he lived.

"We would not intrude if it were not of the utmost importance," the tallest of the three said, his even, formal tone drawing Roger's eyes.

It was then that Roger fully observed the three who stood before him. The woman was petite, quite attractive, with a sense of steel in her eyes. The shorter of the two men had dark, almost black hair and was rather unassuming, average almost. The taller man sent a chill down Roger's back. He was very tall, enough to stand out in almost any crowd. Extremely handsome, not that Roger was a great judge of that, but he had an ethereal quality to him Roger couldn't place. His eyes widened at a random thought. *Could it be?*

"May we enter?" the tall one asked, adding a bow at Roger's jerky nod.

The three filed past Kai and stood in a line by the kitchen as he closed and quickly locked the door. The snap of the last lock seemed final, the rasp of the chain sliding into place sending another shiver down Roger's spine. He stood in silence as Kai crossed to stand with the others. They stood like bookends on either side of the young couple, almost as guards. The realization of who might stand before him in his dingy, cluttered apartment raced through Roger's mind. Butterflies raged to life in his stomach and a flush of embarrassment lit his face.

He took a breath to speak but before he could utter a word, Kai said, "Relax, my friend, and please sit."

"I regret our intrusion, but we could not afford to stand outside exposed for too much longer," the tallest one spoke, his formal, elegant tone sending Roger's heart soaring.

Roger nodded, not trusting himself to speak as he settled in his chair. He couldn't contain himself and continued to fidget, watching as Kai and the tall one began a hurried, whispered conversation. *Could this be an angel Kai spoke of earlier?* Roger couldn't help the feeling of awe overwhelming him.

"He has gathered everything, just as I said. We can leave immediately," Kai whispered, glancing at Roger where he sat.

"Good. Does he know about us?"

"He doesn't know who you are, any of you."

"But he does suspect," Roger interrupted from where he sat in his chair.

He grinned at the shocked expressions as the two spun to face him. "Hearing aids."

All four smiled at that, the shorter man going a step further to actual laughter. His laugh and smile utterly changed him. There was no way he could ever be considered average the way his attitude changed the room. Roger felt lighter, happier, just hearing it.

Roger, pleased with surprising the four, looked at the tallest one. "Tell me."

The tall man gazed at Roger a moment and then spoke. "I am As'hame. It was I Mkai, whom you know as Kai, came to with the same news he told you when last you met. We have begun the search as he explained. These two journey with us."

"Why?"

"Rie gathers information, much as you gather equipment, for which we thank you," As'hame said with a nod of his head that was almost a bow. "Paul is her friend and companion."

Roger felt captivated at the formality of As'hame's speech but he noticed the startled look appearing on Paul's face and the small flush on Rie's. He nodded at the two. *Interesting.*

"We are pressed for time or I would explain more," said Mkai.

"No need." Roger said as he struggle to stand.

Paul rushed to help him. "Let me."

"Th-thank you" Roger said taking Paul's arm, glad, for once, for the aid. "I've assembled what you asked. What else c-can I do?"

"That is all we require for now, unless you know of a safe location? We are expecting others to join us and need someplace secure," As'hame said.

Roger shook off the strange warmth he felt as he stood. "I do, actually," he said. "I set it up years ago for me. It's yours."

"Thank you does little to show our gratitude," As'hame said, bowing. "Truly, Mkai, he is even more resourceful than you said."

Roger waved his hand, dismissing the gratitude, and moved toward the dresser standing by the short hallway. He felt a warmth flush through his body again, but had no idea what it meant. "Here are the keys to the place, and here," he said, tossing first the keys to Mkai then a bigger object, "So you can call me."

Mkai caught the cellphone in his hand and nodded with a smile, "Thank you. It appears you've thought of everything."

"Not everything," As'hame said. "It may no longer be safe for you here, Roger. Do you have some other place you can stay, a friend or relative who might have space for you?"

Roger felt a stab of apprehension.

"Some of my other contacts have been attacked," Mkai said. "I don't think you are known, as I took special precautions, but it might be safer if you left." Roger saw both the fear and sorrow in Mkai's eyes. He surveyed the small apartment that had been his home such a long time then shrugged.

"Yes."

"Wait. That quickly?" Paul said. "Is it so easy to leave your home?"

"Of course. My friend says it's not safe." He sighed. "When you get to my age, a place is just a place, young man. The things that make a home, you carry with you. I'll find somewhere else to hang my hat."

"Do you have a car?"

"No, I can drive, but I don't have much use for a vehicle."

"Then here, you need one." Paul pulled out his keys, separating the unnecessary from what he needed from the bunch. "My car is sitting right outside on the curb. Here's the key and the alarm fob.

You are more than welcome to it. It even has a full tank of gas." The last he said with a smile as he handed the keys over.

"Thank you," Roger said, accepting the keys, touched at the thoughtfulness and kindness in this stranger's eyes. There was something about him Roger just couldn't put his finger on. Something special. But he had no time to think about it now. It was evident Mkai was really worried, and this, more than anything else, got through to Roger.

"Let me show you how to get to the house." he said dragging out a map and quickly marking out the fastest route.

"Don't take too long, Roger. I think you're safe, but I could be wrong." Mkai's brows were drawn tight with concern.

"Don't worry." Roger started unlocking the door. He had a feeling something of great importance was happening here, right here in his home. He didn't want to be the one to delay them or stand in their way.

"I'm serious," Mkai said, placing his hand on his shoulder.

Giving none of his inner thoughts away, Roger swung the door open. "I'll be okay."

He nodded as Paul and Rie moved past him then stood tall as As'hame stopped in front of him.

"Again, we thank you for your help. It has made our task much easier," As'hame said, formally clasping Roger's hand. A surge of joy Roger couldn't deny ran through him and tears started in his eyes.

"And safer," Mkai added, stepping up to his friend.

With a final nod at Roger, As'hame collected Paul and Rie and started to move toward the stairs. "We will wait for you downstairs. Be quick."

Paul stopped to shake Roger's hand. This time, the jolt of warmth was unmistakable. "You have my everlasting gratitude," the young man said. "I will remember. Please, be safe."

Roger couldn't speak around the lump in his throat. Rie paused as she passed Roger, touching his arm and whispering, "Thank you."

Mkai turned to Roger. "Please take care, Roger. Thank you again. I can't tell you how much this means." Mkai held out his hand.

Roger, disdaining the outstretched hand, clasped him as a brother. Mkai stiffened for a moment and then clasped Roger back. After a moment, Roger stepped back and smiled. Mkai gripped his shoulder and squeezed, then nodding one last time, stepped through the door. Roger slowly closed it as Mkai moved toward the stairs.

CHAPTER TWENTY-FOUR

Mkai stepped out of the stairwell, the morning sunlight streaming through the door harsh in the gloom. He joined As'hame where he stood with Paul and Marie by the open doorway.

"I'm ready, thank you for waiting."

"You are welcome," As'hame said. "His aid will make a big difference."

"He seemed really nice." Rie said touching Mkai on the arm, "I like him."

"Me too," Paul said, holding Rie's hand.

"Shall we go? The empty lot is just down the street and, according to the map, it'll probably take a half an hour or so to get to the safe house. There is not a lot of traffic this early."

"Sounds good. Who wants to drive?" Mkai asked, jangling the keys Roger had given him.

"You will drive, I will navigate. Paul and Rie, I would like you in the back." As'hame waited until they all nodded and led them toward the door.

Mkai ran into the angel's back when he abruptly stopped just before stepping outside.

"What is it?" Mkai asked rubbing his nose. *It's like hitting a brick wall.*

As'hame just held up his hand, head cocked to the side. Nerves started dancing in Mkai's stomach as As'hame turned and looked at him. The look of indecision and unexpected grief in his eyes cut at Mkai.

"Trouble. I can sense demons coming this way, packed close enough I cannot make out how many."

"We have to get Roger!" Mkai said, turning to the stairs.

"There is no time. There are too many for me to fight if it comes to that. And if even one gets close enough to sense Paul, our battle will be over before it has begun."

As'hame's words fell like doom, and Mkai's heart twisted in his chest. "Then I'll stay. We can't leave him."

"I need you to help me keep the two of them safe. I am sorry, Mkai."

"But isn't there something we can do?" Rie asked, concern and worry twisting her face.

"It's not right to leave him here defenseless," Paul said, "especially since they probably followed us here."

"I am sorry, all of you. And if there was something we could do, believe me, I would jump at it. My entire existence has been about protecting Man from demons. But Paul's safety comes first. The risk is simply too high. We have no time for this." As'hame said looking sternly at them, "If they even sense Paul might be who they are searching for, we will be mobbed. Mkai will be tortured and killed for betraying them. I will also, for being who I am. Rie they will take and torture and rape, and they will use her to break you, Paul. Twist you and break you until you lose yourself. And the world will be lost. There. Is. No. Time."

Mkai met As'hame's steady gaze for a moment and then bowed his head in defeat. *He's right, there is no choice.* "Ok, let's go."

As'hame nodded and led them out at a run. "Keep up. We need to get out of sight."

"But . . ." Rie started and cut off as Mkai pushed her and Paul to the door.

"Go, there is no time. GO!" Mkai tried to keep the heartache and anger out of his voice but, judging from the compassionate look Paul gave him, he failed. *Roger, I am so sorry. Please forgive me.*

Mkai followed the three onto the street, more by feel than sight, with tears obscuring his vision. He fought the urge to look back, knowing that he would turn back to save Roger if he did. He focused on Paul and Rie in front of him, holding hands as they ran. As'hame darted into the abandoned lot and turned and beckoned them on.

"Hurry! We have to get out of sight!"

Paul and Rie pushed a little harder and followed him in as he slipped out of view. As'hame pulled an old, ragged tarp off a black Ford Explorer. Paul and Rie dragged piled refuse from around it. As'hame turned as Mkai entered the lot.

"Give me the keys and I'll check it; I need you to keep watch."

Mkai nodded and tossed the keys to him and then turned and carefully peeked around the corner. His heart clenched looking at the building of one of his oldest friends, the urge to run back almost overwhelming. *Be safe Roger. Run, run while you can.* He barely heard the rustling behind him as the others cleared the vehicle, his fight against darting back across the street taking his entire attention.

"Mkai, quickly."

As'hame's whispered command pulled him around. Paul swung the rear door shut and passed a shotgun to As'hame. Rie looked up at him from checking the Glock in her hand as Mkai joined them.

"Paul and Rie will ride in the back; I will ride in the front with you," As'hame said as Paul passed him a box of shells. "Keep the weapons out of sight on the floor. Hopefully we will not need them. Drive carefully, do not speed or dart in traffic. Try to merge with what traffic there is."

"Don't stand out. Got it." Mkai said as As'hame passed him the keys. "Let's get out of here."

He slid behind the wheel, pulling his seatbelt on as he started the vehicle. A quick glance showed everyone belted in and he backed the Explorer around and eased it into the alley. *Be safe, Roger.* Mkai drove slowly down the alley and, looking both ways, pulled onto the road leading away from his friend. Three pairs of eyes watched the streets as he took random turns, working to keep under cover until there was enough traffic to blend in. They all breathed a little easier when he turned onto North Vermont Avenue.

"Take Los Feliz to San Fernando Road, avoid the freeway," As'hame said, pointing up the street.

"I'll take Burbank over to Reseda."

"That would work." As'hame nodded, sitting back and relaxing a bit.

As'hame watched the traffic, his head constantly moving, searching, Paul and Rie's whispered conversation a murmur from the backseat as Mkai drove through early morning traffic.

"I am sorry we had to leave him, Mkai," As'hame said quietly, eyes still roaming, "If there had been an alternative I would have taken it."

"I know," Mkai said, heart aching in his chest.

"When we get someplace safe we will check on him. I promise."

"Thank you. How will the others find us?" Mkai said, changing the painful topic. "How long are we going to stay there?"

"They'll be able to sense the area of the city I am in and the neighborhood and so on. How long we stay depends on several factors."

"Like?" Mkai said, braking slowly at a light. "How quickly reinforcements get here?"

"Exactly. Staying stationary, at least at this point, is too dangerous. We will not be able to stay for long, a couple days probably."

"And then what?"

"That depends on how many As'rai get here and when they arrive. Optimally, it will be up to the Council, but we need to get Paul to someplace safe, someplace we control. We will likely move in stages from location to location, gathering more As'rai as we move across country. I know we cannot stay here."

"After that?" Mkai asked. "What does the future hold for Paul and Rie?"

"I honestly do not know. I cannot see that far," As'hame said, meeting Mkai's gaze. "There is more involved in this. I have a feeling this situation is going to get very big, very quickly."

Mkai glanced in the mirror where Paul and Rie were lost in conversation. "Do you think it's going to spread across the world? Like the first time?"

"I think it is likely. He was sent for a reason." As'hame paused. "His time as a regular man is over."

Mkai looked at Rie where she sat beside Paul, worry obvious on her face but her feelings for Paul there for him to see as well. *What will this mean for her?* He shook his head. *Life is going to get very complicated.*

"Turn into that Walmart parking lot." As'hame said.

"Okay," Mkai said, changing lanes and slowing for the turn. "Why?"

"We are getting close to the neighborhood and I want to make sure we are not being followed."

Mkai looked at him, sweat breaking out on his forehead. "Do you sense someone?"

"No, they faded when we left Roger's neighborhood. But they have the ability to mask their presence so it is worth double checking."

Mkai nodded and drove into parking lot, making his way to the far end, weaving up and down the aisles, hoping to confuse anyone watching them. He backed into an end stall for a clear sightline.

"Perfect, watch for anyone that might stand out." As'hame said bending and looking along the line of cars.

"Um, since we're here, do you think we could pop in and pick up some things?" Paul asked from the back.

"Yeah, we have nothing. I'm wearing the clothes I went to work in," Rie added.

Mkai watched As'hame mull over the question for a moment. "Ok, this is as good a place as any. Mkai, you stay here and watch; I will take them in. It will be a quick trip." The last he directed to the two in the back.

"Ten minutes should be all we need," Paul said, unhooking his seatbelt.

"Ok. Mkai, we will not be long." As'hame said reaching for the door.

"Wait one sec," Rie said, digging in her purse. "Put our cell numbers in the one that Roger gave you. We can check everything is clear before we come out."

"Good thinking, Rie, thank you," As'hame said. "Sometimes, I do not think about technology and possibilities."

Mkai looked down at his phone, their numbers beside Roger's, the only other number in the phone. He fought the urge to call and check on him. It wouldn't accomplish anything. He was either safe or he wasn't. *Please be safe.* It would have to wait. He watched the three others walk down to the entrance, As'hame almost a foot taller than both Paul and Rie. Other than that, they didn't stand out from the early crowd. *They should be safe enough, and As'hame is with them.*

With that last thought, he turned back to watch the street and the traffic. It seemed just normal traffic, nothing out of the ordinary in either the cars driving by or the shoppers walking past. He slid down in his seat, sliding it back a bit so the steering wheel wouldn't jam his chest, and settled down to watch. Minutes later, he was already bored and his legs were starting to fall asleep. *This is nothing like the movies.* He let his mind compare his current activity with all the movies and

TV shows he had watched. *Definitely not the same.* He grinned to himself. *But then, what cop show has angels and demons in it?*

The cell phone in his hand buzzed softly and he picked it up, flipping the screen open.

"Clear?" was all the text said.

He glanced around then texted back. "It's good. I'll pick you up at the door."

He sat up, sliding his seat back in position and started the engine. With a final glance, he pulled out and headed to the entrance.

Rie was the first out the door, followed by Paul pushing a cart of bags, As'hame in the rear, head swiveling. Mkai popped the doors and started looking round, keeping an eye out while Paul and Rie threw the bags in the truck and got into the backseat. As'hame, with a final glance, slid into the passenger seat.

"Everything clear?" he asked, buckling in.

"Yes, we're good."

"Ok, take as many side roads as you can, we need to get under cover."

"Will do." Mkai said pulling away from the curb. The first step had begun.

CHAPTER TWENTY-FIVE

Roger settled back in his chair, thinking. Mkai had wanted him to leave but he couldn't with his mind whirling as it was. He couldn't help the way he kept replaying how As'hame and Mkai had stood on either side of the couple, as though standing guard. The short introduction of the two did nothing to answer who they were or why they were travelling with As'hame and Mkai. But they were important, that was unmistakable.

They were also very much connected. He doubted anyone else, even the two themselves, really noticed how often they touched and looked at each other. It was a subtle, unconscious habit for both and, if he wasn't mistaken, one that was fairly new. He hadn't survived this long, got to his age, without the ability to read people well. And everything he picked up about the couple screamed their connection and their importance. He let his mind dwell upon the problem, trying to pick it apart to determine who they might be.

There was definitely a connection between Mkai and the woman as well. He said she gathered information but there was more than just that connection between them. And her companion. Where did the man come in? Who was he? Why was he travelling with them? Obviously, he was more than just a friend of hers. Roger observed a watchfulness, a deference, apparent in both Mkai and As'hame whenever they had looked at Paul. Who was he? *And why did I feel that rush of warmth when he touched me?*

The knock on the door broke his concentration and he felt the thought starting to form break apart like mist and fade away. Something which happened more often as he got older. The knock sounded again as Roger slowly stood up. The thought it might be Mkai and the others, possibly in trouble, made him hurry. Ignoring the peephole, he slipped the chain free and quickly unlocked the door.

"Kai?" He said as he swung the door open.

He froze in shock at the half-dozen forms filling the hallway. He had a moment to register the horns jutting from their foreheads and the black tips of their claws before they rushed the door. The impact sent it crashing open and rebounding back. Roger had a moment of fleeting hope it would swing shut but the creature in the lead caught it and held it open.

He backed away, stumbling in haste as fear gripped him. The demons slowly filled the room, their misshapen forms a disordered mob intruding upon the peace of his apartment.

Focus! Watch and think!

He shoved the fear away, realizing that if he was going to get out of this he had to set his terror aside and concentrate. The door closing had the sound of doom to it as the demons spread about his apartment. One gnarled form, slightly larger and thicker bodied than the others stopped in front of him as the others started destroying his apartment. The sound of furniture being torn apart, of dishes smashed on the floor and walls almost drowned out the demon's sibilant whisper.

"You don't seem as shocked to see us in our true forms as you should be," it rasped, "that tells me something in itself."

It paused and leered, the jagged tooth-filled grin giving the impression of a hungry shark. "You will be anxious to tell us the rest."

"You will get nothing from me," Roger said.

"My name is Ranil, and yes, yes we will."

The certainty in the creature's voice sent shivers down Roger's back and he struggled to keep his hands from shaking. He swallowed hard as the demon stepped close and sniffed.

He leaned in and whispered, "You smell of fear. Fear and death." Roger shrank back in disgust as he felt the demon's forked tongue slide across his cheek.

"The combination makes you taste delicious," the creature said, leaning back, "and it has been awhile since we have fed."

Despair took root as they dragged Roger to his chair. Two demons stood behind him and gripped his arms, pulling them back, the unfamiliar stretching causing bolts of pain to shoot across his shoulders. Roger grunted in pain as the demons twisted his arms further back, shoving his shoulders forward. He was finding it hard to breathe, the uncomfortable position putting pressure on his chest.

"We are going to take our time with you, old man," Ranil said, crouching beside Roger. "This building is empty so there will be no one to hear you scream."

The sharp burning pain as the demon traced a line down across his cheek brought tears to Roger's eyes and he felt something warm trickle down his face. At first the salty tang made him think of tears until Ranil brought his hand up. The bright red blood dripping from his claw drove home the hopelessness of his situation and Roger began to pray, making peace with the death he felt sure was not far away.

He closed his eyes as the agony began, bearable at first and then worsening. Roger lost himself in the suffering, hoping for death to take him even as the demons around him rejoiced. The cracking snap as they broke each finger was barely audible over their cavorting, his tears and sobs lost in the slow flow of blood as it dripped onto the floor. He kept his eyes closed as he felt them wrench off his slippers and pull off his socks. Roger clenched his jaw against the pain he knew was coming.

"Where shall we put this, I wonder?" Ranil whispered in Roger's ear.

Roger's eyes popped open as he felt something smooth and cold slide against his cheek. He shivered when Ranil held up a long metal skewer. He looked past it into the demon's cold, slitted eyes and knew despair. There was no compassion, no life in those eyes. Evil glared back at him, evil delighting in pain and blood.

The last flicker of hope slipped away and Roger closed his eyes, knowing the agony of the last moments of his life would eclipse all the joys and pleasures he had ever experienced. He fought to keep hold of his memories, clinging to what little shards of light he could focus on. The sharp stinging pain as the skewer was shoved under a toenail pulled a cry of pain from him and was met with laughter from the demons around him. A tear spilled from beneath his tightly closed eyes as Ranil twisted the skewer free and shoved it under the next toe.

"Ah yes, ten toes you have and each will feel this sting before I'm through," the demon laughed. "We shall see just how much you can take, human."

Pain washed over him in waves, cresting as the skewer was shoved under the nail of each toe. When Ranil started on his other foot Roger entertained the brief hope he might pass out from the excruciating sensation, but it skittered away as Ranil pulled the skewer free. When the expected jab of pain didn't happen right away, Roger forced an eye open. Ranil smirked at him and slowly lifted the skewer to his mouth. Roger shook his head and quickly closed his eyes, but he wasn't fast enough to stop the image of Ranil's curling, forked tongue sliding and gathering the blood dripping down the skewer from being imprinted on his brain. Roger tried desperately to pull an image from the depths of his memory, anxious to replace the ghastly image of the demon feasting on his blood.

"Should I take your eyes next?" Ranil asked, his sibilant voice a whisper in Roger's ear.

The threat pulled him back and he couldn't stifle the groan as agony hit him all at once. He slowly forced his eyes open, grimacing as jolts of torment coursed through his body. He froze as the tears cleared from his vision and he recognized the claw hovering in front of his eye.

"If I take your eyes will you talk then?"

"I don't know anything!" Roger blurted, fear of losing his sight overriding his vow to say nothing.

Whatever Ranil was going to say was lost in the smash of glass and the splintering of the door. The demons whirled, facing one direction then the other as surprise and shock took hold. Howls of fear filled the air and the creatures fought one another in their terror to escape the five As'rai moving into the room, weapons drawn.

"As'rai!" Their ancient battle cry filled the air as they struck, green blood spraying the air as blades swept down and across, slashing and tearing.

"They are too late for you!" Ranil cried, turning back to Roger and drawing the dagger hanging at his side.

Roger watched the dagger as it was raised high and began to fall. He sent up a quick prayer, regret filling his heart. As the moment of death approached, his mind cleared and he recaptured the thought he had lost earlier. Paul. There was only one reason Roger could think of for the behavior he saw. *They found Him.* He smiled and closed his eyes. *They found Him.*

When the piercing death he expected didn't happen, Roger opened his eyes and met the demon's gaze. The confusion filling them brought comfort to Roger and he smiled again when a blade crashed into Ranil's side, throwing him in a spin to the ground. His arms freed from the grasp of demons, Roger watched, the sudden silence of the room broken by the gurgle of life as it slipped away from his tormentor. Roger worked up saliva and spat on the demon sprawled before him. He raised his head and saw five As'rai gathered in front of him. Green blood stained their blades and splashed across their armor. Roger struggled to focus on the leader, pain crashing in waves over him.

"I am So'tow." the As'rai said. "Be at ease."

It took moments for the words to make sense, their meaning lost in a whirl of agony. Roger could barely credit his senses as he saw the archaic armor, broad swords held in hands seeming too elegant for their power. Calm, beatific faces with the glory of white wings sweeping the air behind them made him rejoice in who stood before him. Angels. He glanced around at the bodies strewn about. Unexpected rescue had come on their swift wings and plucked him from the very jaws of death. Roger struggled to contain his awe, threatening to overcome him, fought to be worthy of the risk they had taken.

"We cannot stay long. We are on an urgent mission," the angel spoke gently, kneeling to one side. "What can we do for you?"

"So'tow, we must go. We have delayed long and must join the others in the search."

The elegance of the words and the formality of how they were spoken seemed so familiar. Roger realized why and he couldn't help blurting out in surprise, "As'hame!"

The stillness descending made him fear, for a moment, he had somehow said something wrong.

"How do you know that name?" So'tow asked, leaning towards Roger.

"They just left," pain and awe filling his voice, "I gathered supplies and equipment for them."

"So'tow?" An angel interrupted, urgency crossing his face.

"I know, but perhaps he can aid us in finding them. Time is something we do not have." The tall angel turned back to Roger, "Do you know where they are going?"

"Yes. A safe house," he paused, realizing the stutter he had had all his life was seemingly gone. *Paul.* "A safe house I found for them."

"Then I, for one, am glad that my scouts sensed the gathering of demons and we arrived in time to rescue you." The sudden smile from So'tow eased Roger's pain. But still, Roger could not contain the grimace of pain as he tried to rise.

"Hold a moment," So'tow said quietly, pushing Roger back into the chair. "Have a sip, only a sip, mind you, of this."

The silver flask felt warm and surprisingly light as So'tow pressed it gently to Roger's lips. There was no taste at all to the liquid as he drank the tiniest sip possible. The warmth spreading through him surprised him and he had to fight the urge to take another sip. The pain started to fade as So'tow tucked the flask in behind his belt and stood, holding his hand to Roger.

"We do not have a lot of time. Are you able to give us directions to this safe house?" So'tow asked.

Roger nodded and taking the offered hand, carefully stood up. The pain wracking his body had eased to a manageable ache as he stood beside the angels who had saved him. Grateful and shocked, Roger couldn't quite stem the tears of relief. Whatever these being wanted from him, he would do his best to provide.

"I can show you the location on a map," he said walking to the kitchen and picking up the map he had used to show As'hame and the others.

"Thank you. It is important that we catch up to As'hame as quickly as possible," So'tow said, following him to the kitchen.

CHAPTER TWENTY-SIX

"The Council decided, Co'tul," So'tow said quietly.

"He has no claim, he leads no La'sfo. Who is he to be honored so?" Co'tul's angry outburst echoed in the small bedroom of Roger's safe house where he, As'hame, and So'tow had gathered. So'tow had arrived soon after As'hame and they hadn't even had a chance to get reacquainted before Co'tul appeared with Ro'molr and Ti'raon. The meeting had been joyous at first but deteriorated quickly when So'tow passed along new orders from the Council.

"It is the Council's will. Are you going to respect their word?" So'tow said, anger thickening his words. "Your choice is this: stay and honor As'hame as M'hablis, or refuse and you can take your squad and be gone."

"Wait. That is not necessary," As'hame said. "He does not have to bend so."

"Yes, it is. Your title has been decreed and bestowed upon you by me, by direct order of the Council, in whose name I do act. He will acknowledge it, or he will be sent away." So'tow paused. "And he will have to answer for such behavior."

The threat was obvious as So'tow stared at Co'tul, the power of the Council apparent in his stance. "He will give over or will be held accountable. In this, the Council will brook no insolence, not from anyone."

"I submit," Co'tul finally uttered after several tense moments, his words low as he bowed his head. "I will follow M'hablis, and will obey, though it mean my destruction."

As'hame sighed in frustration. He had never wanted the authority of leadership. It was why he had refused to lead a squad of La'sfo for so many years. M'hablis had never even occurred to him.

"I accept you, Co'tul, and by action and word will live up to the honor."

Co'tul refused to meet the eyes of either one of the angels and stomped from the room.

"We may have trouble with him," So'tow murmured. "He has always been prideful."

"He is still As'rai, and that is all I need to know," As'hame said.

So'tow nodded and, squeezing As'hame's shoulder, walked out. As'hame sighed. *This is not what I wanted. I never wanted to dictate behavior to others.* He allowed himself a moment to feel self-pity and then chuckled. This was too important for him to want anyone else to be in charge. He followed So'tow down to the living room, not surprised to see the others gathered there, waiting. So'tow and Co'tul had separated to opposites sides of the room, Paul and Rie sitting close together on the couch with Mkai perched on the arm. Ti'raon stood against the wall nearest Paul where she could see the whole room. Ro'molr occupied the other chair, a beer in his hand, his long legs stretched out before him. A bandage wrapped around his neck, disappearing into the collar of his jacket. They all turned and focused on As'hame when he entered the room.

"We're safe now?" Rie asked.

"For now, yes, but we will not be able to stay here indefinitely," As'hame said. "As Ti'raon, Ro'molr, and Co'tul reported, our enemy is drawing closer."

"The attack on Roger shows just how close," Mkai said

"Yes, exactly. Roger was very lucky So'tow and his team arrived when they did. We all were. But it shows how critical time is. We cannot stay here; we need to move and move fast. But where? That is the question we must answer first. Where can we go? The Council is too far and we are too few."

"Vegas," Co'tul interjected. "My team and I have kept the city safe and it would be a good central location for all to gather."

"Perhaps. But Las Vegas is also very crowded," Mkai said. "We may have trouble keeping track of everyone."

Co'tul glowered at Mkai, contempt thick in his voice. "Who are you to question me, demon? They may accept you, but I do not, nor do I trust you. You have no voice here."

"He has a voice as much as any of us," As'hame said. "If not for him, we would be unaware of the threat and our cause could already have been lost. Las Vegas is one option, where else?"

Mkai smiled gratefully at As'hame and leaned back. It was obvious to As'hame that he was more than a little frightened of Co'tul and ill-at-ease in a room of angels.

"We could head north? Into Canada?" Ro'molr suggested with a shrug and then grimaced and gingerly rubbed his shoulder.

"I worry about the distance required to get us all there," said As'hame, shaking his head. "It has to be close enough we can drive quickly and safely."

"We may be out of time," Mkai said, jumping up and rushing from the room.

As'hame led the others as he followed Mkai to the back yard, getting there just as an angel landed.

"M'hablis, demons approach from the south, at least fifty in number," the scout said, dropping to one knee in a quick bow.

As'hame opened his mouth to speak and stopped as another As'rai streaked in from west quickly followed by one from the east who stumbled, so great was his rush.

"Demons, M'hablis, from the east."

"As well as the west!"

"Gather everyone, we must move quickly." As'hame said motioning to the house, "Scouts, I need you to return and keep watch. We move in five minutes. Be back here by then."

As one, the warrior angels bowed, clenched fists over hearts, and leapt into the air, the hard sweep of their wings a loud clap in the silence. As'hame watched them streak away and turned back to the house. His first priority was to make sure Paul and Rie were kept safe.

As'hame watched as Mkai briefly stopped So'tow in the door to the kitchen.

"Thank you very much for helping Roger to safety. You have my most sincere gratitude," Mkai said as So'tow passed on his way to the kitchen.

So'tow paused. "He sacrificed much for us. His safety was important and he needed time to heal. He would not get that here. And we could not carry him regardless."

He nodded at Mkai's smile and continued into the kitchen.

As'hame was more and more impressed with the demon as time went on and events unfolded. Mkai's concern for his human friend touched the angel. "Mkai, Roger is likely safer where he is than with us but your concern for your friend does you honor."

He bowed once to the surprised demon and continued on to the kitchen.

"We should attack them. Why are we running?" Co'tul said as As'hame entered.

"One, because our M'hablis commands it, and two, because the safety of Paul and Rie come first," So'tow said.

"And three, we would be outnumbered by more than three times our number and this is not a battlefield I would choose," As'hame added, joining the two.

"But to run from them," Co'tul said, his voice thick with anger and disgust.

"You will have your chance. This war has barely started," As'hame said. "There will be battle enough for all before it is through."

Co'tul nodded with a surly grunt and left the kitchen, calling his La'sfo as he went.

"We are ready M'hablis. You, the two humans, and Mkai will ride in the SUV. Co'tul and his La'sfo will guard the front and left and mine will guard the right and the rear. We will keep you safe," So'tow said turning to his commander.

"I know you will. The possible fate of the world lies in that man in the front room. His safety is paramount."

So'tow bowed and left, calling his own squad of La'sfo to him. As'hame surveyed the kitchen. The house had been safe for a small handful of hours. Already on the run, the mission to keep Paul out of danger could be more difficult than any of them realized.

He entered the living room to find Paul and Rie standing with their hands entwined.

"Everything is packed in the SUV. We're ready to go," Mkai said, striding through the front door. "There is no sign of any demons yet."

"We are ready," Rie said.

Paul met As'hame's gaze calmly, surprising the angel. *Perhaps he is starting to accept.*

"Then let's go," the angel said, and led them from the house.

As'hame sensed Paul slow as they approached the SUV and turned to face him.

"I know our group seems small, especially against the number of demons approaching," he said as they gathered around him. "But we will keep you safe, Paul, both of you. Trust in us."

He waited until Paul and Rie nodded and he gestured toward the truck.

"Paul, you and Rie in the back seat. Mkai, you are driving."

"Where he goes, so go I."

As'hame was not at all surprised to hear Ti'raon speak up.

"I was not allowed to protect him before; I cannot stand by yet again."

"Of course, Ti'raon. I could not refuse you this. I would have asked it of you anyway." How could he deny her? As'hame understood her burning need to protect Paul, especially in light of her past.

She smiled gratefully and slid in, pulling Paul into the middle of the seat.

"And I? Where do you need me, M'hablis?" Ro'molr said with an irreverent grin, even now.

"I need your eyes, my friend. In the air, half a block in front. So'tow and Co'tul will be screening out at least a block; I need you closer."

"As you wish."

As'hame watched him leap in the air and then turned to Mkai standing to the side. "Are you ready, Mkai?"

"Yes."

"Good. Here, you are driving again." Mkai flinched as As'hame tossed the keys to him.

"You're sure?"

"Yes. I never picked up the skill, I never had the need. It is up to you to get us safely away."

"No pressure or anything."

As'hame just smiled and slid into the passenger seat as Mkai moved around to the driver's side.

"Hang on, this could get a little crazy," he said cranking the engine over even as he clicked on his seat belt.

The guard angels took to the air in a whir of wings as the SUV peeled away from the curb and raced down the street. The angels formed up and spread out to ring their charge, eight sets of scouts streaking in and assuming their positions with their comrades. All were focused on one task. Get them clear and safe.

No one noticed the speeding pickup as it careened down the street, the driver, obviously drunk, barely able to keep it from slamming into cars parked on either side. His veering, wrenching path down the street caught all unprepared. Mkai's attention was focused on the road in front and As'hame didn't notice it until it was too late.

He barely had a moment to shout, "Look out!" before the pickup slammed into their back end, the impact crushing the luggage area and warping the door.

The SUV was thrown into a skidding spin, facing the opposite direction. As'hame forced his door, standing as Ti'raon pushed hers open. She pulled Paul out behind her and stood guard as Rie followed to stand beside him. As'hame nodded and moved to the other side of the stricken vehicle where Mkai was struggling with the crushed door.

"Hold on," As'hame said and tore the door from the rumpled frame and tossed it to the street.

The flight of angels landed in a ring around them as Mkai stepped out beside As'hame. "We can't go on in that!" Paul cried. The skewed back end, tires punctured by wrenched metal, made it clear this vehicle was going nowhere.

"We have no time. Run!" Mkai cried, pointing at demons appearing from a few blocks away.

"Calmly," As'hame said, gripping Mkai's shoulder.

He quickly reviewed the map in his head then pointed up the street "Go that way. Co'tul we need you in the air. So'tow, you and yours are rearguard. I am on point. Ti'raon, Ro'molr you take either side. Go!"

Everyone scattered and As'hame led the way in a controlled jog to the abandoned lot he remembered from the map.

"This is the spot." As'hame said stopping their escape as they arrived at the fenced lot. "Mkai, take them in."

Mkai nodded and led Paul and Rie further into the lot, searching for a more defensible and hidden spot.

"Ro'molr, with me. Ti'raon and Co'tul, take four and hold that small gap in the fence and the rest of us will hold this one," As'hame said.

The six As'rai quickly ran to take up positions blocking the gap while As'hame assessed those left grouped around him.

"Though we are few and the horde pursuing us is many, we are mighty and the love of God is still ours. Remember that as you battle. They are anathema in the eyes of God and, thus, ours to deal with. It falls to us to mete out the punishment God decreed millennia ago." He inhaled deeply and drew his sword, his wings stretching out behind him, "Remember, you fight for God and for His Son. Let us send them back to Hell!" The last came out in a shout as he held his sword aloft and, releasing his hold, let his aura shine forth.

His brethren matched his shout and the empty lot rang with the sound of steel mixed with song as they drew their swords. They turned and waited for the horde, confident in their leader and their cause. The demons would not pass.

CHAPTER TWENTY-SEVEN

The horde flooded down the alleys and roads, their snarls and howls of rage echoing through the silence. As'hame took a few steps away from the angels behind him and stood waiting. Paul watched as they focused on As'hame standing in the alley. His solitary glow separated him from the wall of As'rai behind him. As'hame held forth his sword and beckoned the fiends on. The As'rai waited calmly as the creatures charged. Mere feet away, As'hame dropped his sword as the As'rai behind him gave voice to their battle cries. As one, they let their auras shine free. Blinded, the first rank of demons stumbled and their charge faltered for moment. Long enough for As'hame to lead the first strike against the enemy.

Paul gripped Rie's hand tightly in his and saw, for the first time, the grace and power his self-appointed protectors had to offer as they tore into their enemies. The screams of rage and hate tearing at the air were suddenly filled with fear and pain as monster after monster fell under the righteous wrath of God's soldiers. They watched the angels risking their existence form a slim wall between the ravening beasts and their prey.

Paul stood, astonished, as the scant few As'rai first held firm against more than three times their number and then began to take the battle to those who waited. He still couldn't believe the events of the past few hours, and he wasn't sure he believed what they thought of him—who the angels believed him to be. Was he worth this kind of bloodshed? He watched, keeping any sign of his inner turmoil inside as the angels took a step, and then another, into the flood before them.

Rie smiled beside him when the As'rai began to sing. Their clear voices raised their song to the heavens as they went on the offensive and waded into the waves before them. Joy rang in the air as they fulfilled the role for which they were created; God's soldiers finally faced a worthy enemy in a just cause. Their deadly elegance filled Paul with awe even as it broke the resolve of the monsters, terror taking over and those that could, turning to flee.

Paul shared a glance with Rie and over her shoulder with Mkai. The seeming ease with which the As'rai beat back the demons gave hope to their mission. If these few could win against so many, surely the risk was not so great. The fiends crowded against one another, desperate in their attempts to keep away from the darting blades of the angels. They fell to the angels as the blessed ones fought and sang, As'hame leading the As'rai as they slowly pushed the attackers. Paul watched as As'hame led his small force against the crush of scaled monsters threatening them all. The snarls and yowls of fear were barely audible, an undertone to the heart-lifting song as the angels sang.

The monster leaping from the roof surprised everyone as it fell upon Paul, knocking the two of them to the rear of the lot. Paul rolled free, struggling to his feet, facing the demon's tooth-filled grin as it rose to stand in front of him.

"You're mine, mortal." it said drawing a dagger from its belt.

The demon's harsh voice sent chills down Paul's spine. He saw past it to Rie and Mkai where they had been knocked sprawling. Paul shifted his feet, turning his left side to the creature. He carefully slipped out the Glock, desperately trying to remember what little

As'hame had told him about demons. On this plane, like the angels, they were as mortal as he; bullets could hurt, could kill. The one standing in front of him stood over six feet tall and his thick muscled body told Paul hand-to-hand would be a mistake. A big mistake.

His cat-slit eyes reminded Paul of Mkai's true form but, unlike the friend he was coming to trust, this demon's eyes were filled with anger and madness. He ran the dagger across his arm and held it up to Paul. The green blood bright on his red scaled arm pulled Paul's eyes as the creature advanced a step toward him.

Mkai leapt at the demon with a shout. The demon contemptuously backhanded Mkai, slashing with the dagger in his fist.

"No!" Paul screamed at the blood spraying free as Mkai fell with a cry.

Rie ran to pull Mkai to safety as the demon drew closer. Paul swung the gun up and fired a shot in the air.

"Come on then. You can't be scared of a little gun," he said, taunting the demon. *Keep him distracted.*

"Your soul will be mine," the demon roared and leapt at Paul.

Paul had time to fire once. The demon barely flinched when the round punched through his shoulder before crashing into Paul. He felt the gun knock free from his grasp and narrowly deflected the knife's thrust. Paul was able to turn the knife arm away and tried desperately to keep the creature's snapping maw from sinking into his neck. They stumbled across the rubble in a halting dance, fighting to keep on their feet.

An errant kick sent the Glock sliding across the ground in a clatter of metal on stone. Desperation touched Paul as his hands started slipping from where they gripped the creature's muscled forearm. His eyes darted around, trying to see where the gun went but the glint of sunlight on the blade kept drawing his eyes away. The fiend grunted in pleasure as his immense power slowly twisted the knife toward Paul. Paul flicked his eyes to where Rie knelt with Mkai, his heart twisting at the fear in her eyes. The thought of her being hurt lent strength to his aching muscles and he forced the knife away.

"You seem different, mortal," the thing rasped, forked tongue sliding across Paul's cheek, "The As'rai seem bound to protect you. Is our search over? Have we found you?"

Paul struggled to keep the terror from his face, desperation feeding strength to muscles pushed to their limits.

"If you are who we seek then you are safe, we are not here to hurt you. Simply give over and I will take you away from all this. My brothers will soon break through. I would hate one of them to kill you, lost in blood fury," he growled, forcing Paul further back. "Stop fighting me. My mistress wants to meet with you. To talk with you. That is all. You will be safe, I promise."

"Not likely, demon!" Paul grimaced and renewed his struggle to push the demon back.

Despair twisted at him, *As'hame must be wrong. Jesus would just banish this demon back to Hell. I'm sorry, Marie. I'm just a regular man.*

He saw Ti'raon break free from where she fought with Co'tul and rush toward him. Hope gave him strength enough to twist the knife away.

"Never, demon; you and your kind have no place here and never would I trust anything you say," Paul snarled back and, with a burst of strength, shoved with all his might.

The creature twisted free and shoved Paul hard. He spun backwards, stumbling, to trip and land in the rubble of concrete and stone at the back of the lot.

"Then you will die." The twisted from growled and took a step toward Paul.

He shook his head, trying to keep the darkness at bay, disoriented. His heart soared as Ti'raon dove and rolled to her feet in front of him. The look of surprise and fear that spread over the demon's reptilian face made Paul smile.

"You picked the wrong prey. He is under my protection. You should have stayed in the Hell you came from," Ti'raon said as she drew her own dagger. "But do not worry, you will be home soon."

The demon backed away from the angel standing between him and Paul, his eyes darting around.

"He is claimed by my mistress, angel," he hissed with contempt. "She wants Him alive and I will deliver Him. My brothers may not be so careful. Do you want to risk what the others may do to Him?"

Ti'raon just shook her head with disdain as she drew her dagger. "Neither you nor any of your ilk will ever lay another hand on Him. Not while I stand between you."

"Then die first!" He let out a howl of fear and anger and leapt at the As'rai.

Paul watched as Ti'raon easily slipped past the thrusting dagger. She pushed the demon's arm past her and with a twist spun him around, looping her arm around his throat. She pulled him back against her, off balance, at her mercy.

"You should have listened." she whispered as she thrust her dagger between his ribs.

He convulsed once with a sharp cry of pain, arching high on his toes. Ti'raon let the body collapse in a heap at her feet as she pushed her arms to the sky and tilting her head back, let out the battle cry of the As'rai. Dropping her arms, she quickly walked to Paul's side and held out an arm to help him to his feet. Paul grasped her arm looking past her.

"Ti'raon!" he cried as a gunshot rang out.

Ti'raon spun as he pointed. The battle, seemingly over moments ago was now a struggle. Demons crushed against the As'rai, desperation evident as As'hame battled against the sheer number. Ro'molr was on one knee, hand pressed to his shoulder, holding himself up with his sword thrust into the ground. White cloaked forms of angels lying still on the ground tore at Paul's heart. A demon stood up on the roof, taking aim on the angels at its feet.

"Ti'raon!" Paul cried.

Before the words had left his mouth, her dagger had left her hand, flashing through the air to sink into the demon's chest. It cried out as it fell, hands convulsing on the gun in its hands, bullets crashing harmlessly into the wall of the alley. More demons started to crawl up the walls, trying to get above the battle. Paul saw Co'tul battling desperately, holding the gap alone, his comrades fallen at his feet.

"Ti'raon! He can't hold them!" Paul said, pointing.

Ti'raon turned, desperation on her face. He could tell she was torn between protecting him and defending the wall.

"Go, he needs you," Paul urged, getting to his knees.

Ti'raon nodded and stepped toward Co'tul. At that moment, with a cry of triumph, a group of demons broke through. Three mobbed Co'tul, his sword thrusting as the rest rushed past, trampling the two fallen As'rai. The demons howled and charged toward Ti'raon and Paul where he knelt on the ground.

"As'hame!" Paul yelled.

The angel spun at Paul's cry, taking in the situation at a glance. He took a step, half-crouching, beginning his leap in the air when a demon jumped on his back. Then another, and one more. As'hame dropped to one knee, twisting and shoving, trying to push free of the demons surrounding him. The line of As'rai started to fracture as So'tow led a handful to free his leader. Ro'molr struggled to his feet, blood streaming from his shoulder, as he staggered to Co'tul's aid.

"NO!" Paul shouted as Rie darted from Mkai's side and stood in the path of the charging demons.

The first demon lifted its sword as it came at Rie where she stood, frail, vulnerable and weaponless, willing to give everything in the hope of Paul's survival.

"NO!" This time, the cry came as if wrenched from his very soul.

No more! Paul swept his arm toward the charging demons, fear and desperation tearing at him as, with his very soul, he rejected what he saw unfolding before him.

A radiant stream of light burst from his hand, his entire body vibrating as music and song filled the air. The charging horde faltered, screaming in agony. Weapons fell as clawed hands grabbed at pain-filled heads. Mouths gaped open as they threw their heads back and howledto the heavens. Unbearable grief and loss flowed through the cries as the demons turned and fled en masse. The last of them disappeared as Paul slowly lowered his arm and stared at his hand.

Ti'raon reached to help Paul to his feet, unspeakable joy spread across her face.

Where just seconds ago the din of battle reigned, there was now profound silence.

Paul shook his head. "What was that? I thought . . . I thought I heard music?"

"I heard it too, and laughter," Rie said, kneeling beside Mkai in the dirt, shock filling her voice.

As'hame limped forward with Co'tul, supporting Ro'molr. "That was the light and song of Heaven. As your cities have the ever present hum of electricity and civilization, so does Heaven echo with God's love."

"But what happened?" Paul asked, confused and feeling drained.

"You are the Son of God. One of your gifts is to call and share the light of Heaven. For Man, and angel, it brings joy and peace. For demons, intolerable pain, mixed with grief for what they betrayed and lost."

"But, I heard the music and laughter, too," Mkai said quietly, heartache thick in his voice as he struggled to sit up, blood dripping from the gash in his side.

"You choose to be a part of the Army of Light, and risked your life for it. That is your reward." As'hame said, then turned and placed his hand on Paul's shoulder, eyes full of compassion.

"Now, do you believe?"

******************** END ********************